PATTY'S SUITORS

Carolyn Wells

1st WORLD
LIBRARY
Literary Society

Patty's Suitors

Carolyn Wells

© 1st World Library – Literary Society, 2005
PO Box 2211
Fairfield, IA 52556
www.1stworldlibrary.org
First Edition

LCCN: 2004195591

Softcover ISBN: 1-4218-0412-3
Hardcover ISBN: 1-4218-0312-7
eBook ISBN: 1-4218-0512-X

Purchase *"Patty's Suitors"*
as a traditional bound book at:
www.1stWorldLibrary.org/purchase.asp?ISBN=1-4218-0412-3

1st World Library Literary Society is a nonprofit
organization dedicated to promoting literacy by:

- Creating a free internet library accessible from any computer worldwide.
- Hosting writing competitions and offering book publishing scholarships.

Readers interested in supporting literacy
through sponsorship, donations or
membership please contact:
literacy@1stworldlibrary.org
Check us out at: www.1stworldlibrary.ORG
and start downloading free ebooks today.

Patty's Suitors
contributed by Tim, Ed & Rodney
in support of
1st World Library Literary Society

CONTENTS

I. A VALENTINE PARTY 7

II. ON THE TELEPHONE 21

III. THE HEPWORTHS AT HOME 36

IV. A PERFECTLY GOOD JOKE 51

V. THREE PICTURES 66

VI. PRINCESS POPPYCHEEK 79

VII. SUITORS 95

VIII. A HOUSE PARTY 109

IX. EDDIE BELL 124

X. QUARANTINED 139

XI. MEETING IT BRAVELY 153

XII. A SURPRISE 166

XIII. SISTER BEE 181

XIV. KENNETH 195

XV. AN INVITATION 210

XVI. BELLE HARCOURT 225

XVII. MAY-DAY 240

XVIII. MOONLIGHT 255

XIX. IN THE RUNABOUT 269

XX. THE RIDE HOME 283

CHAPTER I

A VALENTINE PARTY

"It IS a boofy frock, isn't it, Nansome?"

Patty craned her head over her shoulder, as she waited for her stepmother's response, which was only, "Yes."

"Oh, my gracious, Nan! Enthuse! Don't you know half the fun in life is enthusiasm?"

"What shall I say?" asked Nan, laughing.

"Oh, say it's a peach! a hummer! a lallapaloosa!"

"Patty, Patty! what language!"

"Oh, yes; I forgot I meant to stop using slang. But when any one is so lukewarm in her admiration as you are, forcible language is called for."

"Well, it certainly is a lovely gown, and you never looked prettier. There! since you are fishing for compliments, are you pleased now?"

Patty was far from being conceited over her pretty face, but she honestly liked admiration, and, indeed, she was accustomed to receive it from all who knew her. At the present moment, she was standing before a long mirror in her boudoir, putting the last touches to her new party toilette. Louise, the maid, stood by, with a fur-trimmed wrap, and Patty drew on her long gloves with a happy smile of anticipation.

"I just feel sure I'm going to have a good time to-night," she said; "it's a presentiment or premonition, or whatever you call it."

"Don't flirt too desperately," said Nan, not without cause, for pretty Petty was by nature a coquette, and as she had many admirers she merrily led them a dance.

"But it's so interesting to flirt, Nancy. And the boys like it, - so why not?"

Why not, indeed? thought Nan. Patty's flirtations were harmless, roguish affairs, and prompted by mischief and good nature. Patty was a sweet, true character, and if she teased the young men a bit, it was because of her irrepressible love of fun.

"And this is St. Valentine's night," went on Nan, "so I suppose you think yourself privileged to break all the hearts you can."

"Some hearts are so brittle, it's no fun to break them," returned Patty, carelessly, as she adjusted her headdress.

She was going to a Valentine party, where the guests were requested to come in appropriate costume.

So Patty's gown was of white lace, softly draped with white chiffon. On the modish tunic were love-knots of

Carolyn Wells

pale blue velvet, and a border of tiny pink rosebuds. The head-dress, of gold filigree, was a heart pierced by a dart; and on Patty's left shoulder, a dainty little figure of Cupid was wobbling rather uncertainly.

"You'll lose that little God of War," said Nan.

"I don't care if I do," Patty answered; "he's a nuisance, anyway, but I wanted something Valentinish, so I perched him up there. Now, good-bye, Nancy Dancy, and I expect I'll be out pretty late."

"I shall send Louise for you at twelve, and you must be ready then."

"Oh, make it one. You know a Valentine party is lots of fun."

"Well, half-past twelve," agreed Nan, "and not a minute later!"

Then Louise wrapped Patty in a light blue evening cloak, edged with white fur, and the happy maiden danced downstairs.

"Good-bye, Popsy-Poppet," she cried, looking in at the library door.

"Bless my soul! what a vision of beauty!" and Mr. Fairfield laid down his paper to look at his pretty daughter.

"Yes," she said, demurely, "everybody tells me I look exactly like my father."

"You flatter yourself!" said Nan, who had followed,

and who now tucked her hand through her husband's arm. "My Valentine is the handsomest man in the world!"

"Oh, you turtle-doves!" said Patty, laughing, as she ran down the steps to the waiting motor.

Unless going with a chaperon, Patty was always accompanied by the maid, Louise, who either waited for her young mistress in the dressing-room or returned for her when the party was over.

"Shall you be late, Miss Patty?" she asked, as they reached their destination.

"Yes; don't wait for me, Louise. Come back about half-past twelve; I'll be ready soon after that."

Louise adored Patty, for she was always kind and considerate of the servants; and she thought Louise might as well have the evening to herself, as to be cooped up in a dressing-room.

The party was at Marie Homer's, a new friend, with whom Patty had but recently become acquainted.

The Homers lived in a large apartment house, called The Wimbledon, and it was Patty's first visit there. Miss Homer and her mother were receiving their guests in a ballroom, and when Patty greeted them, a large crowd had already assembled.

"You are a true valentine, my dear," said Mrs. Homer, looking admiringly at Patty's garlanded gown.

"And this is a true Valentine party," said Patty, as she

noted the decorations of red hearts and gold darts, with Cupids of wax or bisque, here and there among the floral ornaments.

Marie Homer, who was a pretty brunette, wore a dress of scarlet and gold, trimmed with hearts and arrows.

"I'm so glad to have you here," she said to Patty; "for now I know my party will be a success."

"I'm sure your parties always are," returned Patty, kindly, for Marie was a shy sort of girl, and Patty was glad to encourage her.

As soon as the guests had all arrived St. Valentine appeared in the doorway.

It was Mr. Homer, but he was scarcely recognisable in his garb of the good old Saint.

He wore a red gown, trimmed with ermine, and a long white beard and wig.

He carried an enormous letter-bag, from which he distributed valentines to all. They were of the old-fashioned lace paper variety, and beautiful of their kind.

Mrs. Homer explained that on the valentine of every young man was a question, and the girl whose valentine had an answer to rhyme with it, was his partner for the first dance.

The young men were requested to read their valentines aloud in turn, and the girls to read their responsive answers.

This proceeding caused much hilarity, for the lines were exceedingly sentimental, and often affectionate.

When it was Roger Farrington's turn, he read out boldly:

"Where's the girl I love the best?"

and Marie Homer, who chanced to hold the rhyming valentine, whispered, shyly:

"I am sweeter than the rest!"

"You are, indeed!" said Roger, as he offered his arm with his courtliest bow.

Then Kenneth Harper read:

"Who's the fairest girl of all?"

and Mona Galbraith read, with twinkling eyes:

"I'll respond to that sweet call!"

Then it was Philip Van Reypen's turn. He glanced at his valentine, and asked:

"Who's a roguish little elf?"

Everybody laughed when a tall, serious-faced girl responded:

"I guess I am that, myself!"

It was toward the last that Clifford Morse asked:

"Who's the dearest girl I know?"

and as Patty's line rhymed, she said, demurely:

"Guess I am, - if YOU think so!"

"I'm in luck," said Clifford, as he led her to the dance. "You're such a belle, Patty Fairfield, that I seldom get a whole dance with you."

"Faint heart never won fair lady," laughed Patty, shaking her fan at him. "I always accept invitations."

"Accept mine, then, for the next dance," said Philip Van Reypen, who overheard her words as he was passing.

"No programmes to-night," returned Patty, smiling at him. "Ask me at dance time."

As no dances could be engaged ahead, except verbally, Patty was besieged by partners for every dance.

"Oh, dear," she cried, as, at the fourth dance, five or six eager young men were bowing before her; "what shall I do? I'd have to be a centipede to dance with you all! And I can't divide one dance into six parts. And I can't CHOOSE,-that would be TOO embarrassing! Let's draw lots. Lend me a coin, somebody."

"Here you are," said Van Reypen, handing her a bright quarter.

Patty took it, and put both hands behind her.

"You may try first , Phil , because you put up the

capital. Right or left?"

"Right," said Philip, promptly.

Patty gaily brought her hands into view, and the quarter lay in her left palm.

"Next!" she said; "Mr. Downing."

"Left," chose that young man, as Patty again concealed her hands.

But that time she showed the coin in her right hand.

"My turn now," said Ken Harper, "AND, you'll please keep your hands in front of you! You don't do it right."

"Do you mean that I cheat?" cried Patty, in pretended rage.

"Oh, no, no! nothing like that! Only, this game is always played with the fists in view."

So Patty held her little gloved fists in front of her, while Kenneth chose.

"Right!" he said, and her right hand slowly opened and showed the shining coin.

"Were you going to take me, anyway?" asked Kenneth, as they walked off together. "And why did you turn down poor Van Reypen? He was awfully cut up."

"Ken Harper, do you mean to insinuate that I didn't play fair?"

Carolyn Wells

"Yes, my lady, just that. Oh, cheating never prospers. You have to put up with me, you see!"

"I might do worse," and Patty flashed him a saucy glance.

"I wish you meant that."

"Oh, I do! I DO, Ken. Truly, there are lots of worse people than you in the world."

"Who?"

"Well, - there's Eddie Perkins."

"Oh, Patty! that fop! Well, I'll bet you can't think of another."

"No; I can't."

"Patty, how dare you! Then you'll sit right here until you can."

Laughingly Kenneth stopped dancing, and led Patty to an alcove where there were a few chairs. As they sat down, Philip Van Reypen came toward them.

"Oh, Ken," Patty cried, "I've thought of a man worse than you are! Oh, EVER so much worse! Here he is! And I simply adore bad men, so I'm going to dance with him."

Naughty Patty went dancing off with Van Reypen, and Ken looked after them, a little crestfallen.

"But," he thought, "there's no use being angry or even

annoyed at that butterfly of a girl. She doesn't mean anything anyway. Some day, she'll wake up and be serious, but now she's only a little bundle of frivolity."

Kenneth had been friends with Patty for many years; far longer than any of her other young men acquaintances. He was honestly fond of her, and had a dawning hope that some time they might be more than friends. But he was a slow-going chap, and he was inclined to wait until he had a little more to offer, before he should woo the pretty butterfly.

And, too, Patty would never listen to a word of that sort of thing. She had often proclaimed in his hearing, that she intended to enjoy several years of gay society pleasures, before she would be engaged to any one.

So Kenneth idly watched her, as she circled the room with Van Reypen, and took himself off to find another partner.

"Oh, Valentine, fair Valentine," said Van Reypen to Patty, as they danced.

"Wilt thou be mine, and I'lt be thine," returned Patty, in mocking sing-song tones.

"Forever may our hearts entwine," improvised Philip, in tune to the music.

"Like chickwood round a punkin-vine," Patty finished.

"Pshaw, that's not sentimental. You should have said, Like sturdy oak and clinging vine."

"But I'm not sentimental. Who could be in a crowded

ballroom, in a glare of light, and in a mad dance?"

"What conditions would make you feel sentimental?"

"Why, - let me see. Moonlight, - on a balcony, - with the right man."

"I'm the right man, all right, - and you know it. And if I'm not greatly mistaken, here's moonlight and a balcony!"

Sure enough, a long French window had been set slightly ajar to cool the overheated room, and almost before she knew it, Patty was whisked outside.

"Oh, Philip! Don't! you mustn't! I'll take cold. I ought to have something around me."

"You have," said Van Reypen, calmly, and as he had not yet released her from the dance he held his arms lightly round her shoulders.

Patty was angry. She knew Philip loved her, - several times he had asked her to marry him, - but this was taking an unfair advantage.

The February wind itself was not colder than the manner with which she drew away from him, and stepped back into the ballroom.

"My dear, my dear," exclaimed Mrs. Homer, who chanced to be near, "how imprudent! You should not go out without a wrap."

"I know it, Mrs. Homer," and Patty looked so sweetly penitent that her hostess could but smile at her. "But, truly, I just stepped out a single second to get a tiny breath of air. The room IS warm, isn't it? May I stay here by you a few moments?"

"Yes, indeed," and Mrs. Homer drew the girl down beside her on the sofa. "You're not robust, my child, and you mustn't run foolish risks."

"You're quite right, and I won't do it again. But on a night not quite so cold, that balcony, flooded with moonlight, must be a romantic spot."

"It is, indeed," said Mrs. Homer, smiling. "My young people think so; and I hope you will have many opportunities in the future to see it for yourself."

"Your young people? Have you other children besides Marie?"

"Yes; I have a daughter who is away at boarding-school. And, also, I have a nephew, whose home is in this same building."

"Is he here to-night?"

"No; Kit hates dances. Of course, that's because he doesn't dance himself. He's a musician."

"Kit? What a funny name."

"It's Christopher, really, Christopher Cameron; but he's such a happy-go-lucky sort of chap, we naturally call him Kit."

"I think I should like him," said Patty. "Would he like me?"

"No," said Mrs. Homer, her eyes twinkling at Patty's look of amazement. "He detests girls. Even my daughters, his cousins, are nuisances, he says. Still he likes to come down here and sit on my balcony, and tease them. He lives with his parents in the apartment just above us."

"He sounds an interesting youth," said Patty, and then, as Roger came up and asked her for a dance, she promptly forgot the musical nephew.

At supper-time, Patty's crowd of intimates gathered around her, and they occupied a pleasant corner of the dining-room.

"What'll you have, Patsums?" asked Roger, as a waiter brought a tray full of dainty viands.

"Sandwiches and bouillon," said Patty, promptly; "I'm honestly hungry."

"The result of exercise in the open air," murmured Philip Van Reypen, as he took a seat directly behind her.

Patty gave an involuntary giggle, and then turned upon Philip what she meant to be an icy glare. He grinned back at her, which made her furious, and she deliberately and ostentatiously ignored him.

"Hello, you two on the outs?" inquired Kenneth, casually.

"Oh, no!" said Philip, with emphasis; "far from it!"

So , as Patty found it impossible to snub such

cheerfulness, she concluded to forgive and forget.

"There's something doing after supper," remarked Roger. "Miss Homer dropped a hint, and even now they're fixing something in the ballroom."

"What can it be?" said Elise, craning her neck to see through a doorway.

"It's a game," said Marie Homer, who had just joined the group. "I told mother, you all considered your-selves too grown-up for games, but she said she didn't want to have the whole evening given over to dancing. So you will play it, won't you?"

"Sure we will!" declared Kenneth, who admired the shy little girl.

Marie was new in their set, but they all liked her. She was timid only because she felt unacquainted, and the good-natured crowd did all they could to put her at ease.

"Games!" exclaimed Philip; "why, I just love 'em! I'll play it, whatever it is."

"I too," said Patty. "It will be a jolly change from dancing."

CHAPTER II

ON THE TELEPHONE

When the young people returned to the ballroom, it presented a decidedly changed appearance. Instead of an interior scene, it was a winter landscape.

The floor was covered with snow-white canvas, not laid on smoothly, but rumpled over bumps and hillocks, like a real snow field. The numerous palms and evergreens that had decorated the room, were powdered with flour and strewn with tufts of cotton, like snow. Also diamond dust had been lightly sprinkled on them, and glittering crystal icicles hung from the branches.

At each end of the room, on the wall, hung a beautiful bear-skin rug.

These rugs were for prizes, one for the girls and one for the boys. And this was the game.

The girls were gathered at one end of the room and the boys at the other, and one end was called the North Pole, and the other the South Pole. Each player was given a small flag which they were to plant on reaching the Pole.

This would have been an easy matter, but each traveller was obliged to wear snowshoes. These were not the real thing, but smaller affairs made of pasteboard. But when they were tied on, the wearer felt clumsy indeed, and many of the girls declared they could not walk in them at all. And in addition each one was blindfolded.

However, everybody made an attempt, and at a given signal the young people started from their opposite ends of the room and endeavoured to make progress toward the goal as they blindly stumbled along.

Patty concluded to move very slowly, thinking this the surest way to make a successful trip. So she scuffled along among the other laughing girls, now and then stumbling over a hillock, which was really a hassock or a sofa cushion under the white floor covering. It was great fun, and the girls cheered each other on as they pursued their blinded way. And then about midway of the room they met the boys coming toward them. Then there was scrambling, indeed, as the explorers tried to get out of each other's way and follow their own routes.

It was a very long room, and Patty hadn't gone much more than halfway, when she concluded to give up the race as being too tiresome. She made her way to the side of the room, and reaching the wall she took off her blinding handkerchief and kicked off the snowshoes. To her great surprise she found that many of the other girls and some of the boys had done the same thing, and not half of the original contestants were still in the race. And, indeed, it proved to be much greater fun to watch those who were still blindly groping along, than to stay in the game.

At last the game was concluded, as Roger Farrington proudly planted his flag at the very spot that designated the North Pole, and not long after, Clementine Morse succeeded in safely reaching the South Pole. So the beautiful rugs were given to these two as prizes, and every one agreed that they had earned them.

Then, amid much laughter, everybody was unblind-folded. and they all sat around on the snow mounds waiting for the next game.

A big snow man was brought in and set in the centre of the room. Of course it was not real snow, but made of white plaster, gleaming all over with diamond dust. But it was the traditional type of snow man, with a top hat on, and grotesque features.

In the mouth of the figure was a cigarette, and each guest was presented with a few snowballs, made of cotton wool. The game was to knock the cigarette from the snow man's mouth with one of the snowballs.

Of course the cigarette was so arranged that the lightest touch of a ball would dislodge it, and as one cigarette was displaced, Mr. Homer supplied another.

The guests had been divided into two parties, and each side strove to collect the greater number of cigarettes.

Some balls flew very wide of the mark, while others with unerring aim would hit a cigarette squarely.

The game caused great hilarity, and everybody was anxious to throw balls. They threw in turn, each having three balls at a time.

Patty was especially deft at this, and with true aim succeeded several times.

Then when they tired of this play, a few more dances followed before it was time to go home.

Some attendants came in and whisked away the snow hillocks and floor covering, leaving the ballroom once again in order for dancing.

"Makes me feel young again, to play those kiddy games," said Kenneth, as he was dancing with Patty.

"I like them," returned Patty; "I hate to think that my childhood is over, and I love games of any kind."

"Your childhood will never be over," returned Kenneth; "I think you are the incarnation of youth, and always will be."

"I'm not so much younger than you."

"Five years, - that's a long time at our age. By the way, when are the Hepworths coming home?"

"Next week; and we're planning the loveliest reception for them. You know their apartment is all ready, and we're going to have just a few people to supper there, the night they return."

"Shall I be one of the few?"

"Well, rather! The best man at the wedding must surely be at the home-coming. Doesn't it seem funny to think of Christine as mistress of her own home? She'll be perfectly lovely, I know. My goodness gracious! Ken, what time is it? I'm afraid I'm staying too late. I promised Nan I'd leave at half-past twelve."

"It's not much more than that. Can't you stay for another dance?"

"No, I can't possibly. I must run right away, or my motor car will turn into a pumpkin, and Louise into a white mouse. Take me to Mrs. Homer, please, and I will say good-night to her."

But as they crossed the room, they met Van Reypen coming toward them.

"Our dance, I think," he said, coolly, as he took Patty's hand.

The music had just started, and its beautiful rhythm was too tempting for Patty to resist.

"I'm just on my way home," she said, "but we'll go around the room once, and then I must go."

"Once indeed!" said Philip, gaily; "we won't stop until the music does."

"Yes, we will; I must go now," but somehow or other they circled the room several times. Patty loved dancing, and Philip was one of the best of partners.

But at last she laughingly protested that she really must go home, and they went together to say good-night to their hostess. And then Patty said good-night to Philip, and ran away to the dressing-room, where Louise was patiently waiting for her.

And soon, muffled up in her furs, they were rapidly spinning along toward home.

"I didn't keep you waiting very long, did I, Louise?" said Patty, kindly.

"No, Miss Patty, you're right on time. I expect you would have liked to stay longer."

"Yes, I should, but I promised Mrs. Fairfield not to."

When at last Patty reached her own little boudoir, she declared she was more tired than she had realised. So Louise took off her pretty frock, and Patty sat in her blue silk dressing gown while the maid brushed her hair. Then she brought her a cup of hot milk, and left her for the night.

Patty wasn't sleepy, and she dawdled around her room, now and then sipping the milk, and then looking over her engagements for the next day.

"Oh," she thought, suddenly, "I've left my fan at the party. I'm sorry, for it's my pet fan. Of course it will be safe there, but I think I'll telephone Marie to look it up and put it away."

Knowing that the Homers would not yet have retired, Patty picked up her telephone and called the number.

A masculine voice gave back a cheery "Hello!"

"Is this Mr. Homer?" said Patty.

"No, indeed. I'm Kit Cameron. Who are you, please?"

"Isn't this The Wimbledon apartment house?"

"It sure is."

"Isn't this 6483?"

"No, it's 6843. Please tell me who you are?"

A spirit of mischief entered into Patty. She knew this must be Marie Homer's cousin, who lived on the floor above the Homers, and who, Mrs. Homer had said, detested girls.

"But I have the wrong number," she said. "I didn't mean to call you."

"But since you did call me, you must tell me who you are."

"I'm a captive princess," said Patty, in rather a melancholy tone. "I'm imprisoned in the dungeon of a castle."

"How awful! May I get a squad of soldiers and come to your rescue, oh, fair lady?"

"Nay, nay, Sir Knight; and anyway you do not know that I am a fair lady."

"Your voice tells me that. Surely such musical tones could belong only to the most beautiful princess in the world."

"Oh, yes, I am THAT," and Patty laughed, roguishly; "but a well-behaved princess would not be talking to a strange man. So I must say good-bye."

"Oh, no, no! wait a minute; you haven't told me your name yet."

"And I don't intend to. You detest girls, anyway."

"Yes, I always have, but you see I never met a princess before."

"You haven't met me yet."

"But I shall! Don't make any mistake about that."

"How can you? I'm going to ring off now, and you have no way of tracing me."

"I can find out from Central."

"No, you can't."

"Why can't I?"

"Because I forbid you to do so."

"All right; then I can't find out that way, but I'll find out some other way. I'll go on a quest."

"Goodness, what is a quest?"

"Oh, it just means that I henceforth devote my whole life to finding you."

"But you can't find me, when you don't know my name."

"I'll make up a name for you. I'll call you Princess Poppycheek."

Carolyn Wells

"How could you guess I'm a brunette?"

"I can tell it from your voice. You have snapping black eyes and dark curly hair, and the reddest of red cheeks."

"Exactly right!" exclaimed Patty, giggling to think how far this description was from her blonde pink-and-white type.

"I knew it was right!" exclaimed the voice, exultantly; "and I shall find you very soon."

"Then I shall await your coming with interest. You prefer brunettes, do you?"

"Well, as a matter of fact, I have always admired blondes more, but I'm quite willing to change my tastes for you. Do you sing?"

For answer, Patty sang softly into the telephone, the little song of "Beware, take care, she is fooling thee."

Although she did little more than hum it, Mr. Cameron was greatly impressed with her voice.

"By jove!" he exclaimed. "You CAN sing! Now, I can find you easily. There are not many voices like that in this wicked world."

"Do you sing yourself? But I don't want to know, I haven't the least interest in a stranger, and besides, I'm going to ring off now."

"Oh, wait a minute! I don't sing, but I do something better. Don't ring off, just listen a minute."

Patty listened, and in a moment she heard a violin played softly. It was played by a master hand, and she heard an exquisite rendition of the "Spring Song."

"Beautiful!" she exclaimed, as the last notes died away, and then suddenly realising that she herself was acting in a most unconventional manner, she said abruptly, "Thank you; good-bye," and quickly hung up her receiver.

For some time she sat thinking about it. Curled up in a big easy chair, her blue silk boudoir gown trailing around her, she sat giggling over her escapade.

"It's all right," she assured herself, "for of course I know who he is, though he doesn't know me. He is Mrs. Homer's nephew, so it's just the same as if I had met him properly. And, anyhow, he hasn't an idea who I am, and he never can find out from the description he has of me!"

Still giggling over the episode, Patty went to bed and to sleep.

The next morning, as she thought it over, she realised that she hadn't succeeded in securing her fan, and she determined to go around and see Marie that afternoon, and get it.

So that afternoon she went to make her call.

"It was a beautiful party," she said to Marie, as the two girls chatted together. "I love games for a change from dancing, and the games you had were so novel."

"I'm glad to hear you say that," said Marie, "for I was

afraid they would seem too childish."

"No, indeed," returned Patty; "and now put on your hat and come out with me for a little while. I'm going to a picture exhibition, and I'd love to have you go too. But first, did I leave my fan here last evening?"

"There was a beautiful fan left here, - an Empire fan. Is this yours?"

Marie produced the fan and Patty recognised it as her own.

"But I can't go this afternoon," said Marie, "because Cousin Kit is coming down to practise some new music. Won't you stay and hear him play? He is really a very good violinist."

Patty considered. She rather wanted to meet this young man, but she was afraid he would think her forward. So after a little further chat, she rose, saying she must go. And it was just as she was going out that Mr. Cameron came in, with his violin under his arm.

Patty was obliged to pause a moment, as Marie presented her cousin, but the young man, though courteous, showed no interest whatever in Miss Fairfield. Patty's pretty face was almost invisible through her motor veil, and as Mr. Cameron had no idea that she was the girl who had talked to him the night before, and as he really had no interest in girls in general, he merely made a very polite bow and went directly toward the piano.

"I wish you'd stay and hear some music," said Marie, but Patty only murmured a refusal, not wanting Mr.

Cameron to hear her voice, lest he recognise it.

He was an attractive looking man of fine physique and handsome face, but he looked extremely dignified and not very good-natured.

"All musicians are cross," Patty thought to herself as she went down in the elevator, "and I wasn't going to have that man think that I went around to Marie's to see him!"

She decided to call for Elise to go to the art gallery with her, and she found that young woman ready and glad to go.

"I hadn't a thing to do this afternoon," said Elise, as they started off, "and I love to go anywhere with you, Patty. Shall we have a cup of tea afterwards?"

And so it was after they had seen the pictures, and as they were sitting in a cosy little tea-room, that Elise said suddenly:

"Do you know Mr. Cameron? He's a cousin of Marie Homer's."

"I don't know him," said Patty, smiling, "but I've been introduced to him. Just as I was leaving Marie's to-day, he came in. But he was very abstracted in his manner. He merely bowed, and without a word he went straight on to the piano and began fussing with his music."

"You were just leaving, anyway?"

"Yes; but I would have remained a few moments, if he had been more sociable. But, of course, I couldn't insist on his talking to me, if he didn't want to."

"He doesn't like girls," said Elise, but as she spoke she smiled in a self-conscious way.

"So I've heard," said Patty, smiling herself. "He seems young to be what they call a woman-hater. I thought only old bachelors were that. Well, he has no interest for me. There are plenty of boys in our own set."

"Don't you tell, if I tell you something," and now Elise looked decidedly important.

"What is it? I won't tell."

"Well, it's the funniest thing! That Mr. Cameron wants to meet me, though he never has seen me."

"What!" exclaimed Patty, in astonishment. "Why does he want to meet you?"

"I don't know, I'm sure. But he was at Marie's this morning, and asked her if she knew any girl who was gay and merry and had a sweet voice, and had dark hair and eyes and rosy cheeks. And Marie says she knows he means me, and I think he does too! Isn't it exciting?"

"Yes," said Patty, drily. "But you don't sing much, Elise."

"Oh, of course I don't sing like you do, but I have a fairly decent voice."

"But how mysterious it is. What does he know about you?"

"I don't know. It IS mysterious. He wouldn't tell Marie anything except that he wanted to know the name of the girl he described; and he said she must be friendly enough with Marie to call her up on the telephone in the middle of the night."

"But did you do that?" asked Patty, who was really shaking with laughter.

"Yes; I called her up last night after I got home from the party, because I'd left my spangled scarf there, and I wanted her to put it away safely for me."

"I always leave things at a party, too," said Patty, looking innocent. "I left my fan at Marie's last night. So I went there to-day and got it."

"Well, I thought I'd better telephone, for so many girls leave things and they get scattered or lost."

"Well, what did your telephoning have to do with Mr. Cameron?"

"I don't know; that's the queer part of it. Perhaps the wires were crossed and he heard me talking."

"H'm," said Patty, "perhaps he did. When are you going to meet him, Elise?"

"I don't know; but Marie says she'll have a few friends to tea some day soon, and she'll ask him. She says it'll have to be a very small tea, because he hates to meet people."

"Why doesn't she have just you two? I think it would be more romantic."

"Oh, nonsense. This isn't romance. I think Mr. Cameron is a freak, anyway. But it's all amusing, and I hope you'll be at the tea, yourself, Patty."

"I will if I'm asked," said Patty.

CHAPTER III

THE HEPWORTHS AT HOME

It was the day of Christine's home-coming, and Patty was busy as a bee preparing for the great event. The pretty apartment where the Hepworths were to live was all furnished and equipped, but Patty was looking after the dainty appointments of a party.

Not a large party, only about a dozen of their own set. Nan was there, too, and Elise Farrington, and they were arranging flowers in bowls and jars and vases, till the rooms were a bower of blossoms.

"What time will they arrive?" said Elise.

"We expected them about six o'clock," returned Patty; "but I had a telegram, and their train is delayed, so they can't get here until nine. So I want the party all assembled when they come. It's five now, and everything's about done, so we can scoot home and get some dinner and get dressed, and be back here before they arrive. I'll be here by half-past eight, for the caterers are coming then, and I want to see about the table."

So they all went home to dress, and before half-past eight Patty was back again.

Carolyn Wells

There were two maids already installed, but Patty found plenty to do in superintending matters, and she hadn't much more than completed the decorations of the table, when the guests began to come.

"Isn't the apartment lovely?" exclaimed Mona Galbraith, as she went through the rooms. "This music-room, or living-room, or whatever you call it, is just dear! Who selected the furnishings?"

"Oh, Mr. Hepworth and Christine," said Patty; "two artists, you know; of course the rooms ought to be beautiful. It is a lovely place, and just the right setting for that darling of a Christine."

The whole merry crowd were assembled in the living-room, when the bride and groom arrived. A shout of welcome went up from the young people, and Christine was smothered in girlish embraces, while the men vigorously shook Mr. Hepworth's hand, or clapped him on the shoulder, in their masculine way of congratulation.

Christine looked very sweet and smiling, in a pretty travelling gown, but Patty carried her off at once and insisted that she get into a house gown.

"The idea," said Patty, "of a hostess in a high-collared frock and all her guests in evening dress!"

So Christine quickly changed to a little chiffon gown of pale green and Patty tucked a pink rose in her hair and some more in her belt.

"Now you look like a bride," said Patty, nodding approval at her, and leading her to a mirror; "look at that vision of beauty! Aren't you glad I made you change?"

"Yes, ma'am," said Christine, in mock humility; "it's much better so."

The evening was a merry one. They danced and they sang and they chatted and finally they had the delightful supper that Patty had ordered.

Christine, blushing prettily, took the head of the table, while Gilbert Hepworth, with a proud air of proprietorship, sat at the other end.

Patty, as guest of honour, sat at the right hand of her host.

"It has always been my aspiration," she said, with a beaming smile at Christine, "to have a married friend to visit. I warn you, Christine, I shall spend most of my time here. There's one little nook of a bedroom I claim as my own and I expect to occupy it very frequently. And, besides, I have to give you lessons in housekeeping. You're a great artist, I know, but you must learn to do lots of other things beside paint."

"I wish you would, Patty," and the little bride looked very much in earnest; "I truly want to keep house, but being an artist and a Southern girl both, I don't believe I'm very capable."

"You're a blessed dear, that's what YOU are"; and Patty turned to Hepworth, saying, "Isn't she?"

"Yes, indeed," he returned; "I've only just begun to realise the beautiful qualities in her nature. And it is to you, Patty, that I owe my happiness. I shall never forget what you did in order that Christine might come to New York."

"And now we are surprised at the result," said Patty, who never could be serious for long at a time. "Come on, people, you've had enough supper, let's have one more dance and then we must go home and leave these turtledoves to their own nest."

But the one dance proved to mean several, until at last Patty said, "This will never do! Christine is all tired out, and as the superintendent of this party I order you all to go home at once."

The others laughingly agreed, except Philip Van Reypen, who came near Patty and murmured, "You haven't danced with me once to-night, and you've been awful cruel to me lately, anyway. Now let us have one more dance in honour of the bride's home-coming."

"No," said Patty, firmly, "not another dance to-night."

"Just a part of one, then," begged Philip; but Patty was inexorable.

And so the merry crowd dispersed, Patty lingering a moment to give Christine a good-night kiss and wish her every blessing and happiness in her new home.

"And I have you to thank for it all, Patty dear," said Christine, her blue eyes looking lovingly into Patty's own.

"Nonsense, thank your own sweet self. You well deserve the happiness that has come to you. And now good-night, dear; I'll be over some time to-morrow."

The laughing group went away, and as it had been planned, Mona took Patty home in her car.

"I wish you'd go on home with me, Patsy," said Mona, as they rolled along toward Patty's house.

"Can't possibly do it. I've a thousand and one things to look after to-morrow morning."

"But it isn't late; really it's awfully early. And I'll send you home early to-morrow morning."

"No, I mustn't, really, Mona. I have to look after some things for the Happy Saturday Club, which it won't do to neglect. And I want to run over to Christine's to-morrow morning, too. I have some things to take to her."

"Do you know, Patty, I think they're an awfully humdrum couple."

"Who? The Hepworths? Oh, I don't think humdrum is the right word, - they're just serious-minded."

"But Mr. Hepworth is so old and prosy, and Christine seems to me just a little nonentity."

"Now, Mona, that isn't fair. Just because you are a frivolous-headed butterfly of fashion, you oughtn't to disdain people who happen to have one or two ideas in their heads."

"Well, the only ideas they have are about pictures."

"Pictures are good ideas."

"Yes, good enough, of course. But there's no fun in them."

"That's the whole trouble with the Hepworths. They haven't any fun in them. Neither of them has a sense of humour. But that's good, too; for if one had and the other hadn't, they'd be miserable for life. But as it is they don't know what they miss."

"No, they don't. Patty, don't ever marry a man without a sense of humour."

"Trust your Aunt Patty for that. But I don't propose to marry anybody."

"Of course not; he'd propose to you."

"Funny Mona! Don't let your sense of humour run away with you. Well, this facetious 'he' that you conjured up in your imagination may propose all he likes; I sha'n't accept him, - at least not for many years. I mean to have a lot of fun before I get engaged. Can you imagine me settled down in a little apartment like Christine's, devoting myself to domestic duties?"

"No; but I can fancy you married to a millionaire with two or three country houses and yachts and all sorts of things."

"Good gracious, Mona. I don't aspire to all that! Just because YOU're a millionairess, yourself, you needn't think everybody else longs for untold wealth. After I get pretty well along in years, - I think I shall marry a college professor , or a great scientist. I do love brainy men."

"Well, there are no brainy men in our set."

"Oh, Mona, what a libel! Our boys, - somehow I never can think of them as men, - are quite brainy enough for their age. And at the present day, I'd rather have fun with Ken or Roger, just talking foolishness, than to discourse with this wise professor I'm talking about. But of course, I wouldn't marry Ken or Roger even if they wanted me to, which they don't."

"Oh, yes, they do, Patty; everybody wants to marry you."

"Don't be a goose, Mona; you know perfectly well that Roger is over head and ears in love with you. Of course, I'm mortally jealous, for he was my friend first, and you stole him away from me. But I'll forgive you if you'll let up on this foolish subject and talk about something interesting."

"I will, Patty, if you'll tell me one thing. Don't you like Mr. Van Reypen very much?"

"Phil Van Reypen? Of course I do! I adore him, - I worship the ground he walks on! I think he's the dearest, sweetest chap I ever knew!"

"Would you marry him?"

"Not on your life! Excuse my French, Mona, but you do make me tired! NOW will you be good? We're nearly home and I had a lot of things I wanted to ask you, and here you've been and went and gone and wasted all our time! Foolish girl! Here we are at my house, and I thank you, kind lady, for bringing me safely home. If you'll let your statuesque footman see me in at my own door, I'll promise to dream of you all night."

The girls exchanged affectionate good-nights, and Patty ran up the steps and Louise let her in.

"Nobody home?" asked Patty, noting the dim lights in the rooms.

"No, Miss Patty," answered Louise, "Mr. and Mrs. Fairfield are not in yet."

"Well, I'm not a bit sleepy, Louise, and I'm not going to bed now. I shall stay in the library for awhile, - perhaps until they come home."

Louise took Patty's wraps and went away, and Patty wandered around the library selecting a book to read. The girl was a light sleeper, and she often liked to read a while before retiring.

But after she had selected a book and arranged a cosy corner in a big easy-chair by a reading light, she still sat idle, with her book unopened.

"I don't feel a bit like reading," she thought to herself; "I do hate to come home from a party so early. Of course I could write some letters, but I don't feel like that, either. I feel like doing something frisky."

She jumped up and turned on more lights. Then, chancing to see herself in the long mirror, she bowed profoundly to the pretty reflected figure, saying: "Good-evening, Miss Fairfield, how well you're looking this evening. Won't you sing a little for us?"

Then she danced into the music-room, and sitting down at the piano, sang a gay little song.

Then she sang another, and then looking over some old music she came across the little song, "Beware," that she had sung over the telephone to Kit Cameron. Naturally her thoughts turned to that young man, whom she had almost forgotten, and she wondered if he had met Elise yet.

"That was quite a jolly little escapade," she said to herself; "that young man certainly thought I was a little black-eyed beauty, and when he does see Elise, of course he'll think she's the one. I believe I'll call him up and mystify him a little more. It's all right, because I've really been introduced to him, and if he doesn't remember me, *I* can't help it! Probably he'll be out anyway; but I'll have a try at it."

Returning to the library, Patty sat down at the telephone and called up Mr. Cameron's number.

His own gay, cheery self answered "Hello," and Patty said in a shy little voice, "Is this you, Mr. Cameron?"

"Bless my soul! if it isn't my fair Unknown, again!"

"Why do you call me, fair, when you know I'm dark?"

"Oh, fair in this case means bewitching and lovely. It doesn't stand for tow hair and light blue eyes! and neither do I!"

"But you said you liked blondes."

"I used to, before I knew you."

"But you don't know me."

"Oh, but I do! I know you a whole heap better than lots of people who have seen you. There's something in a telephone conversation that discloses the real inner nature. It was dear of you to call me up to-night. You don't know how it pleases me!"

"Oh, I didn't do it to please you. But I'm all alone in my dungeon tower - "

"Wait a minute; what IS a dungeon tower?"

"Oh, don't quibble. Anyway, I'm all alone, and I simply had to have some one to speak to."

"How did you know I'd be here?"

"Be there! Why, I assumed that you sat at your telephone every evening, waiting to see if I would call you!"

"You little rascal! That's exactly what I have done, but I don't see how you knew it. Are you still a captive princess?"

"Yes; they keep me on bread and water, and not very much of that."

"Couldn't I come and try to liberate you?"

"No, Sir Knight. Alas, you would but be captured yourself."

"But to be captured in such a cause, would be a glorious fate!"

"Oh, aren't you romantic! I really wish it were the Fifteenth Century, and you could come on a dashing charger, and rescue me with a rope ladder! I'm simply dying for an escapade!"

"All right; I'll be there in a few minutes!"

"No, no! it's just five centuries too late. Now, one can only meet people in humdrum drawing-rooms."

"And do you think there's no romance left in the world?"

"*I* can't find any." Naughty Patty put a most pathetic inflection in her voice, which touched Mr. Cameron's heart.

"Look here, my lady," he said, "there IS romance left in this old world, and we're IT! Now, this telephoning is all very well, but I'm determined to meet you face to face. And that before long, too."

"Oh, you've been making inquiries about me. You know I forbade that."

"No, you didn't; you only said I mustn't ask Central who telephoned. There was surely no harm in asking my cousin who called her up the other night. And very naturally she told me. So she's going to be the Fairy Godmother who will bring us together by the touch of her magic wand."

" Oh , if you know who I am, the fun is all gone out of

our escapade!"

"Not at all; the fun is only about to begin."

"Then Marie did tell you all about me?" And Patty's tones betokened disappointment.

"She didn't need to tell me much about you. She told me your name, and the rest I want to know about you, I either know already or I shall learn for myself."

"If you know my name, why don't you call me by it?" And Patty had great difficulty to stifle her laughter.

"May I call you by your first name?"

"Not as a regular thing, of course. But if you know it, you may use it just once. But you can only use it to say good-night. For this session is over now."

"But I don't WANT to say good-night. I want to talk to you a long time yet."

"Alas, that may not be. It is even now time for my jailers to visit my dungeon, and if they catch me at this foolish trick, they will probably reduce my allowance of bread and water. And so, if you're going to call me by name, you must do it quickly, for I'm going to hang up this receiver, as soon as I say good-night!"

Patty's positive tones apparently carried conviction that she would do just as she said, for Mr. Cameron sighed deeply and responded, "It is such a beautiful name it seems a pity to use it only once. But I know you mean what you say, so as your liege knight, fair lady, I obey.

Good-night - Elise -"

The name came slowly, as if the speaker wished to make the most of it, and Patty fairly thrust the receiver back on its hook as she burst into laughter. It surely was a joke on the young man! He had asked Marie who was her pretty brunette friend, and Marie had honestly thought he must mean Elise Farrington.

Patty was still giggling when her parents came in from a concert they had been attending.

"What IS the matter, Patty?" asked Nan. "Why do you sit up here alone, grinning like a Chessy cat, and giggling like a school-girl? Were the Hepworths so funny that you can't get over it?"

And then Patty told Nan and her father the whole story of Kit Cameron and the telephone.

Nan laughed in sympathy, but Mr. Fairfield looked a little dubious.

"And I thought you a well-brought up young woman," he said, - half in earnest and half in jest. "Do you think it's correct to telephone to strange young men? I'm shocked! that's what I am, - SHOCKED."

"Fiddlesticks, Fred," said Nan; "it's perfectly all right. In the first place, the man HAS been introduced to Patty. She met him at Miss Homer's."

"But she telephoned BEFORE she met him," stormed Mr. Fairfield, for Patty had told the whole story.

"But she didn't do it purposely," said Nan, impatiently.

"She got him on the wire by mistake. She couldn't help THAT. And, anyway, when he said he was Miss Homer's cousin, that made it all right. I think it's a gay little joke, and I'd like to see that young man's face when he meets Patty!"

"I shan't meet him," said Patty, pretending to look doleful; "he hates tow-headed girls."

"Well, you're certainly that," said her father, looking at her with pretended disapproval. "I have to tell you the truth once in awhile, because everybody else flatters you until you're a spoiled baby."

"Tow-headed, am I?" and Patty ran to her father, and rubbed her golden curls against his own blond head. "And, if you please, where did I inherit my tow? If I hadn't had a tow-headed father I might have been the poppy-cheeked brunette that everybody admires. It isn't fair for YOU to comment on MY tow-head!"

"That's so, Pattikins; and I take it all back," for Mr. Fairfield could never resist his pretty daughter's cajolery. "You are a pretty little doll-faced thing, and I expect I'll have to forgive your very reprehensible behaviour."

"I'm NOT a doll-face," said Patty, pouting; "I shan't let you go until you take THAT back."

As Patty had her arms tightly round her father's neck, he considered it the better part of valour to take back his words. "All right," he said, "rather than be garro-ted, - I retract! You're a beautiful and dignified lady, and your notions of convention and etiquette are above reproach."

"They're above YOUR reproaches, anyhow," returned Patty, saucily, and then she ran away to her own room.

Carolyn Wells

CHAPTER IV

A PERFECTLY GOOD JOKE

Patty decided to do nothing in the matter of meeting Kit Cameron. She dearly loved a joke, and this seemed to her a good one. But she thought it would spoil it, if she made any move in the game herself. So she bided her time, and it was perhaps a week later that Marie Homer came to call on her.

As Marie hadn't the slightest notion that Patty was the girl her cousin had in mind, the subject was not mentioned until just before Marie left, when she asked Patty if she would come to her home the next week to a little musicale.

"Not a big party," said Miss Homer, "just a dozen or so really musical people to spend the evening. And I want you to sing, if you will. My cousin will be there, - the one who plays the violin."

"I thought he detested society," said Patty, her eyes twinkling a little.

"I don't know what's come over Kit," returned Marie, looking perplexed. "He's been the funniest thing of late. He has some girl in his mind -"

"A girl!" exclaimed Patty; "I thought he scorned them."

"Well, I can't make this out. It's awfully mysterious. I think I'll tell you about it."

"Do," said Patty, demurely.

"Two or three weeks ago, - in fact, it was the day after my valentine party, - Kit asked me which of my friends had telephoned me late the night before. You know he lives in the apartment just above ours, and it seems the wires were crossed or something, but he heard this girl's voice, and now he insists he wants to meet her. I don't think Elise Farrington has such a fascinating voice, do you?" "Elise!" exclaimed Patty, in pretended surprise; "what has SHE to do with it?"

"Why," explained Marie, "Elise did call me up that night, to say she had left her scarf. But how Kit discovered that she was a red-cheeked brunette, is more than *I* can understand. You can't know that from a voice, now, can you?"

"No," said Patty, decidedly, "you CAN'T!"

"Well, then, a week or two went by, and I told Elise about this, but somehow I couldn't manage to get them together. Every time Elise came to our house, Kit would be away somewhere. But a few days ago I did manage to have them meet."

"Did you?" exclaimed Patty; "for gracious sake, WHAT happened?"

Marie looked a little surprised at Patty's excited

interest, but she went on: "Oh, it was AWFULLY funny. Elise looked lovely that day. She had just come in from skating, and her cheeks were red and her eyes sparkled, and her furs were SO becoming! I introduced Kit, and I could see he admired her immensely. There were several people there, so I left these two together. They were getting on famously, when Kit said to her, 'Are you still a Captive Princess?'

"I didn't know what he meant, and Elise didn't either, for she looked perfectly blank, and asked him why he said that. And Kit told her she knew well enough why he said it, and Elise thought he must be crazy. However, they got along all right until Kit asked me to get Elise to sing. Now, you know Elise doesn't sing much; she has a nice little contralto voice, but she never sings for people. But do you know, she was perfectly willing, and she sang a little lullaby or something like that, rather sweetly, *I* thought. But such a change came over Kit's manner! I don't know how to express it. He was polite and courteous, of course; but he seemed to have lost all interest in Elise."

"But your cousin IS a sort of a freak, isn't he?" said Patty, who was deeply interested in Marie's story.

"Why, no, he isn't a freak. He's a musician, but he's an awfully nice chap, and real sensible. He hates society as a bunch, but he often likes an individual here and there, and when he does he can be awfully nice and friendly. But this whole performance was so QUEER. He wanted to meet Elise, and when he did, he admired her, I could see that; but when she sang, the light all went out of his face, and he looked terribly disappointed. The girl isn't a great singer, but why in the world should he expect her to be, or care so much because she isn't?"

"It IS strange!" murmured Patty; "how did Elise take it?"

"Oh, I don't think she minded much; she thinks the boy half crazy, anyway; asking her if she was a captive princess! And, of course, he didn't let HER see that he was disappointed in her voice. But I know Kit so well, that I can tell the moment he loses interest in anybody. I'm awfully fond of Kit, - we've grown up more like brother and sister than cousins."

"What's he like? Has he any fun in him?"

"Well, he loves practical jokes, - that is, if they're not mean. He couldn't do a mean or unkind thing to anybody. But he likes anything out of the ordinary. Escapades or cutting up jinks. He and Beatrice, - that's my younger sister, - are always playing tricks on us, when she's at home. But it's always good-natured fun, so we don't mind. Oh, Kit's a dear; but you never can tell whether he's going to like people or not. He likes so very few."

"But he liked Elise?"

"Oh, yes; in a general way. But, for some reason I can't make out, he was terribly disappointed in her."

"And he's going to play at your musicale?"

"Yes; and I want you to sing. We have two or three other musicians, and it will really be rather worth while."

Patty hesitated. If she went to this party, and met Kit, all the mystery of her little romance with him would be ended. He would be more disappointed in her than he had been in Elise, for at least she conformed to his favourite type of beauty, and Patty was quite the reverse. She could sing, to be sure, but probably her voice would not charm him, when robbed of the glamour lent by the telephone.

"Oh, DO say yes," Marie urged; "it will be a nice party, and if I've left out any people you specially want, I'll invite them."

But Marie's list included all of Patty's set, and as she rather wanted to go, she finally decided to say yes.

"Good for you!" exclaimed Marie; "now I know the party will be a success!"

"You always say that to me," said Patty, laughing. "*I* don't make parties a success."

"Yes, you do," said Marie, in a tone of firm conviction; "you're so nice, and pretty, and smiling, and always seem to have such a good time, that it makes everybody else have a good time."

"What do you want me to sing?"

"I don't care at all. Make your own selections. I like you best, I think, in some of those sweet, simple ballads."

"I rarely sing anything but ballads or simple music," said Patty, "my voice isn't strong enough for operatic soaring."

"Well, sing what you like, Patty, if you only come," and Marie went away, greatly elated at having secured Patty's consent to sing at her musicale.

Patty at once went to the piano, and began to look over her music. She smiled as she came across "Beware," but she concluded that would not do for a regular program, though she might use it as an encore.

She made her selections with care, as she honestly wanted to do credit to Marie's musicale, and then, taking several pieces of music, she ran up to Nan's room to ask her final judgment in the matter.

"You'll have a lot of fun out of this, Patty," said Nan, laughing, as she heard the whole story. "When is it to be?"

"Friday night. Do you know, Nan, I'd like to play a joke on that boy, between now and then."

"I think you are playing a joke on him, - and, besides, he isn't a boy."

"No; Marie says he's about twenty-four. He's a civil engineer, besides being a musician. But, anyway, I've got him guessing. I'm glad Elise didn't take it to heart, that she wasn't the right girl,-but Marie says Elise thinks he's a freak, anyway. And, too, I believe he's not very nice to girls as a rule, so of course Elise won't want him. Oh, *I*'M the only girl in the world for him!"

Patty pirouetted about the room on the tips of her toes, waving a sheet of music in either hand.

"What a silly you are, Patty, with your foolishness!"

Patty dropped on one knee at her stepmother's side, and clasping her hands, looked up beseechingly into the smiling face over her.

"But you love silly, foolish little girls, don't you, Nancy Nan?"

"Yes, when they're you," and Nan patted the shining head at her knee.

"Well, very few of them ARE me!"

"Thank goodness for that! I don't know what I'd do if you were a half a dozen!"

"You'd have just six times as much fun in your life!" and Patty jumped up and began to sing the songs she had brought.

Then together they decided on the ones she should sing at the musicale.

Although Patty's voice was not very strong, it was sweet and true and had been carefully cultivated. She sang with much charm, and her music always gave pleasure. She never attempted anything beyond her powers, and so her songs, while selected with good taste, were not pretentious.

That evening, while Patty was fluttering around her room, pretending to get ready for bed, but really dawdling, she was moved to telephone once again to the young man who was fond of jokes.

"It's you, is it?" he almost growled, in response to her call.

"Yes," said Patty, in a meek little voice; "shall I go away?"

"Great jumping cows! NO! Don't go away, stay right where you are!"

"But I'm going away for ever," said Patty, moved by a dramatic impulse; "my captors have found out that I'm holding communication with you, and they're going to take me away to another castle, and imprison me there."

"Stop your fooling; I want to know who you are, and I want to know it quick! Do you hear THAT?"

"Yes, I hear," returned Patty, saucily, "but I don't have to answer! And if you talk to me like that, I shall hang up this receiver."

"I won't talk like that any more. But, do you know, I thought I had found you, and you turned out to be somebody else."

"But I can't be anybody else. I'm only myself."

"Be serious a minute, won't you? I went to my cousin's and met a beautiful, poppy-cheeked princess; but she wasn't you."

"How do you know she wasn't?"

"Because she couldn't sing a LITTLE bit! And you can."

"I can sing a LITTLE bit! Oh, thank you!"

"Now, I want to ask you something. You know my cousin, don't you?"

"Have you sisters and cousins, whom you reckon up by dozens?"

"It doesn't matter if I have. I mean my cousin, Marie Homer, to whom you telephoned, or tried to, on the fourteenth of February. But you got me, instead, and that means we're each other's valentine. See?"

"No, I don't see at all. I only like pretty valentines."

"Oh, I'm as pretty as a picture! That part is all right. Now, I've tried my best to find out who you are, from Marie. But either she can't or won't tell. But I've found out one thing, for certain. You're NOT Miss Farrington."

"No, I'm not; but I never said I was."

"I know you didn't, but you told me you were a pretty brunette, with poppy cheeks, - and Miss Farrington is that."

"Did I tell you I was PRETTY? Oh, I'm SURE I didn't!"

"You didn't have to. I know that myself. Now, if you'll keep still a minute, *I'D* like to speak."

"If I can't talk, I may as well hang up this receiver, for I'm sure I don't want to sit here and listen to you."

"Chatterbox! Now, listen; Marie is having a musicale next Friday night, and I want you to come."

"Without an invitation!" Patty's voice sounded horrified.

"Yes;" impatiently. "Marie would invite you fast enough if she knew who you were."

"Perhaps she HAS invited me."

"No, she hasn't; I saw her list. It's a small party, not more than twenty. And I asked her about each one, and not one of the ladies seemed to correspond to your description."

"Who's going to sing?" asked Patty, calmly.

"Only two ladies; a Miss Curtiss and a Miss Fairfield."

"Perhaps I'm one of those."

"No; I asked Marie, and she says Miss Fairfield is a pretty little blonde, and Miss Curtiss is a tall, brown-haired young woman."

"Don't you know either of these ladies?"

"No; that is, I've never seen Miss Curtiss, but Marie says I met Miss Fairfield one day, for a moment."

"Don't you remember her?"

"Hardly; she seemed an insignificant little thing."

"Pretty?"

"How do I know! She was all wrapped up in motor togs, and acted like a gawky schoolgirl."

"She did! Why, *I* know that Fairfield girl, and she isn't gawky a bit! She's a fascinating blonde."

"No blonde can fascinate ME! MY girl is a poppy-cheeked brunette, and I'm going to catch her before long. Ah, DO come to Marie's party, - won't you?"

"I've never yet gone where I wasn't invited, and I don't propose to begin now. But if you can get Marie to invite me, I'll go."

"Don't be so cruel! I can't do more than I have in the matter. I've teased Marie to death over this thing, and she can't think who you can be, unless you're a Miss Galbraith. You're not, are you?"

"Gracious, no! I'm not Mona Galbraith!"

"I knew you weren't; Marie says SHE can't sing. Oh, dear, you're a perfect torment! Pretty princess, - pretty Princess Poppy-cheek, WON'T you take pity on your humble slave and adorer, and tell me your name?"

"No; but I'll tell you what I will do. I'll send you my photograph."

"Oh, you heavenly angel! You dear, beautiful princess! When will you send it? Don't wait for the morning; call a messenger, and send it to-night!"

"I'll do nothing of the sort. I'll send it to-morrow morning, - by messenger, if you like, - and if you'll promise not to ask the messenger who sent it."

"I'll promise that if you so ordain. I guess I can play cricket!"

"All right then; now listen, yourself. I shall send you three pictures. You pick out the one you think I am, and take it to Marie, and if you are right, she'll invite me. She knows me well enough, but she can't recognise me from your description."

"I don't think it's fair for you to play that way; but I'm dead sure I can pick out your picture from the three."

"All right then; good-night!" And Patty hung up the receiver with a snap.

Then she lay back in her big chair and indulged in a series of giggles.

"Sam Weller says," she said, to herself, "that the great art of letter writing is to break off suddenly and make 'em wish they was more, - and I expect that applies equally well to telephoning."

And she was quite right, for the impatient young man at the other end of the wire was chagrined indeed when the connection was cut off. He was too honourable to use any forbidden means of discovering Patty's identity, and so would not ask to see any telephone records, and was quite willing to promise not to quiz a messenger boy. And so, he could do nothing but wait impatiently for the promised photograph.

Meanwhile Miss Patricia Fairfield was looking over her portrait collection to see what ones to send. She had a box full of old photographs, but she wanted to select just the right ones.

But at last she tumbled them all on the table in a heap, and wisely decided to leave the decision till morning.

And so it happened, that when Nan came to Patty's room next morning, as she often did, she found that coquettish damsel, sitting up in bed, wrapped in a blue silk nightingale, and with a flower-decked lace cap somewhat askew on her tumbled curls.

Her breakfast tray sat untouched on its little stand, while on the counterpane were spread out some twoscore portraits of more or less beautiful maidens.

"What ARE you doing?" said Nan; "playing photograph solitaire?"

"I'm playing a game of photographs," said Patty, raising a pair of solemn blue eyes to Nan, "but it isn't exactly solitaire."

"You needn't tell ME! You're cutting up some trick with that new man of yours." And Nan deliberately brushed away some pictures, and sat down on the side of the bed.

"You're a wizard!" and Patty gazed at her stepmother. "You could have made your fortune, Nan, as a clairvoyant, telling people what they knew already! But since you're here, DO help me out." And Patty told Nan the scheme of the three photographs.

Now, Nan was only six years older than Patty herself, and she entered into the joke with almost as much enthusiasm as the younger girl.

"Shall you send one of your own, really?" she inquired.

"No; I think not. But I want to get three different types, just to fool him."

After much consideration the two conspirators selected a picture of a dark-eyed actress, who was pretty, but of rather flashy effects. Next they chose a picture of an intellectual young woman, with no pretension to beauty or style, and whose tightly drawn black hair and stiff white collar proclaimed a high brow. It was a picture of one of the girls in Patty's class, who had been noted for her intellect and her lack of a sense of humour.

"He'll know that isn't you, Patty," said Nan, objecting.

"No," said Patty, sapiently; "he's pretty clever, that young man, and probably he'll think I'm just that sort. Now for the third, Nancy."

It took a long time to select a third one, for Nan was in favour of a pretty girl, while Patty thought it would be more fun to send a plain one.

At last they agreed on a picture of another of Patty's school friends, who was of the willowy, die-away kind. She was a blonde, but of a pale, ashen-haired variety, not at all like Patty's Dresden china type. The pose was aesthetic, and the girl looked soulful and languishing.

"Just the thing!" cried Patty. "If he thinks I look like THAT, I'll never speak to him again!"

And so, amid great glee, the three pictures were made into a neat parcel, and addressed to Mr. Christopher Cameron.

"Now, for goodness' sake, Patty, eat your breakfast! Your chocolate is stone cold. I'll go down and call a messenger and despatch this precious bundle of beauty to its destination."

"All right," returned Patty, and, with a feeling of having successfully accomplished her task, she turned her attention to her breakfast tray.

CHAPTER V

THREE PICTURES

It was Tuesday morning that Patty had sent the pictures, and that same evening she was invited to dine and go to the opera with Mrs. Van Reypen.

Patty was a great favourite with the aristocratic old lady, and was frequently asked to the Van Reypen home. It is needless to say that Mrs. Van Reypen's nephew, Philip, usually managed to be present at any of his aunt's affairs that were graced by Patty's presence. And, indeed, it was an open secret that Mrs. Van Reypen would be greatly pleased if Patty would smile on the suit of her favourite and beloved nephew.

But Patty's smiles were uncertain. Sometimes it would suit her caprice to smile on Philip, and again she would positively snub him to such an extent that the young man was disgruntled for days at a time.

"But," as Patty remarked to herself, "if I'm nice to him, he takes too much for granted. So I have to discipline him to keep him where he belongs."

The dinner at the Van Reypen mansion was, as always, long and elaborate, and perhaps a trifle dull.

Carolyn Wells

Mrs. Van Reypen's affection for Patty was of a selfish sort, and it never occurred to her to invite guests of Patty's age, or who could be entertaining to the girl.

And so to-night the other guests were an elderly couple by the name of Bellamy and a rather stupid, middle-aged bachelor, - Mr. Crosby. These with the two Van Reypens and Patty made up the whole party.

Patty found herself assigned to walk out to dinner with Mr. Crosby, but, as Philip sat on her other side, she had no fear of being too greatly bored.

But to her surprise the elderly bachelor turned out to be exceedingly interesting. He had travelled a great deal, and talked well about his experiences, and it was soon discovered that he and Patty had mutual friends in Paris, where Patty had spent the winter several years before.

"I do love to hear you talk," Patty declared, ingenuously, after Mr. Crosby had given her a thrilling and picturesque description of an incident in his trip to the Orient.

"Oh, thank you," Mr. Crosby returned, a little bewildered by this outright compliment, for he was unaccustomed to talking to young girls.

"But, you see," Patty went on, "I mustn't monopolise you. You know, it's etiquette to talk fifteen minutes to your neighbour on one side and then turn to your neighbour on the other."

"Bless my soul! you're quite right, - quite right!" and Mr. Crosby stared at Patty over his glasses. "How do you know so much, and you such a young thing?"

"Oh, I'm out," returned Patty, smiling, "and of course, when a girl comes out, she has to learn the rules of the game."

So Mr. Crosby turned to talk to the lady on his other side, and Patty turned to Philip, who looked a trifle sulky.

"Thought you were going to talk to that chap all evening," he growled, under his breath.

"I should like to," said Patty, sweetly, "he's SO interesting. But I can't monopolise him, you know. As I don't want to talk to a growly bear, I think, if you'll excuse me from polite conversation, I'll meditate for awhile."

"Meditate on your sins; it'll do you good!"

Patty opened her blue eyes wide and stared at the speaker. "Why," she said, "to meditate, one must have something to meditate on!"

"And you think you haven't any sins! Oh, would some power the giftie gi'e us!"

"To see ourselves as ithers see us," Patty completed the rhyme. "But you see, Philip, as I don't see any sins in myself, I can't meditate on the sins that ithers see in me, if I don't know what they are."

"Well, I'll tell you a big, black one! You simply ignored me for half an hour, while you jabbered to that duffer on the other side! Now meditate on THAT!"

Carolyn Wells

Patty obediently cast down her eyes, and assumed a mournful expression. She continued to sit thus without speaking; until Philip exclaimed:

"Patty, you little goose, stop your nonsense! What's the matter with you to-night, anyway?"

"Honestly, Philip," said Patty, very low, "your aunt's parties always make me want to giggle. They're heavenly parties, and I simply ADORE to be at them, but her friends are so - well, so aged, you know, and they seem to - well, to be so interested in their dinner."

"*I*'m my aunt's guest, and *I*'m not a bit interested in my dinner."

"Well, you may as well be, for I'm going to talk to Mr. Crosby now."

Seeing that Mr. Crosby's attention was unclaimed for the moment, Patty turned to him, saying, with great animation: "Oh, Mr. Crosby, MAY I ask you something? I'm AWFULLY ignorant, you know, and you're so wise."

"Yes, yes, what is it?" And the great Oriental scholar looked benignly at her over his glasses.

Now naughty Patty hadn't any question to ask, and she had only turned to her neighbour to tease Philip, so she floundered a little as she tried to think of some intelligent enquiry.

"What is it. Miss Fairfield?" prompted Mr. Crosby.

Patty cast a fleeting glance toward Philip , as if

appealing for help, and that young man, though engaged in a desultory conversation, whispered under his breath, "Ask him about the Aztecs."

"Oh, yes, Mr. Crosby," said Patty, "it's about the - the Aztecs, - you know."

"Ah, yes, the Aztecs, - a most interesting race, MOST interesting, indeed. And what do you want to know about them, Miss Fairfield?"

Patty was tempted to say ALL about them, for her knowledge of the ancient people was practically nothing.

"Did they - did they -"

"Eat snails," said Philip, in a whisper.

"Did they eat snails, Mr. Crosby?" And Patty's big blue eyes were innocent of anything, save an intense desire to know about the Aztec diet.

"Snails? - snails? - well, bless my soul! I don't believe I know. Important, too, - most important. I'll look it up, and let you know. Snails - queer I DON'T know. I made a study of the Aztecs, and they are most interesting, - but as to snails -"

Apparently Mr. Crosby's mind was wrestling with the question.

"He's gone 'way back and sat down with the Aztecs," Philip murmured to Patty, "so you ask questions of me."

"You don't know anything that I want to know."

"Then *I'll* ask a question of YOU."

Philip's voice was full of meaning, so Patty said hastily: "No, no; it isn't polite to ask questions in society; one should make observations."

"All right, observe me. That's what I'm here for. Observe me early and often, and I'll be only too well pleased."

"But that isn't what *I'm* here for. Your aunt invited me to be a pleasant dinner guest and so I have to make myself entertaining to my Aztec friend."

And then Patty turned again to Mr. Crosby, and by a few skilful hints she soon had him started on another description of his travelling experiences, and this time it proved so thrilling that all at the table were glad to listen to it.

After dinner the whole party went to the opera and occupied Mrs. Van Reypen's box.

Patty was passionately fond of music, and never talked during a performance. Between the acts, she was a smiling chatterbox, but while the curtain was up, she behaved in most exemplary fashion. Mrs. Van Reypen knew this, or she would not have asked her, for that lady was old-fashioned in her ways, and had no patience with people who chattered while the great singers were pouring forth their marvellous notes.

When the final curtain fell, Mrs. Van Reypen invited her guests to return to her house for supper , but

Patty declined.

"Very well, my dear," said her hostess, "I think, myself, you're too young to be out any later than this. We will set you down at your own door, and you must hop right into bed and get your beauty sleep. Young things like you can't stay young unless you take good care of your pinky cheeks."

"But I don't want Patty to go home," Philip grumbled, to his aunt.

"Your wishes are not consulted, my boy; this is my party. You're merely my guest, and, if you don't behave yourself, you won't get invited again."

"That scares me dreadfully," and Philip lightly pinched his aunt's cheek. "I will be good, so I'll be asked again."

The big limousine stopped at Patty's door, and Philip escorted her up the steps.

"I think you might have come to supper," he said, reproachfully, as he touched the bell.

"It's too late," said Patty, decidedly; "and, besides, I have other plans for the rest of the evening."

And with this enigmatical announcement Philip was forced to be content, for Patty said good-night and vanished through the doorway.

"And, indeed, I HAVE other plans," Patty said, to herself. "I'm simply consumed with curiosity to know which of those three beauties that ridiculous Kit man likes the best. I'm going to call him up and see. I wish he could call me up, - it would suit me far better. But I suppose nobody can call anybody else up if nobody knows anybody else's name."

"Do you want any supper, Miss Patty?" asked Louise, as she unhooked Patty's frock.

"No, thank you, I'm not a bit hungry. You might bring me a cup of milk and a biscuit, and then give me a kimono. I'm not going to bed just yet."

So Louise arranged everything just as Patty wanted it, and finally went away.

"May as well be comfortable," said Patty, as she tucked herself into a favourite big chair, with the telephone on a little stand beside her. "I suppose I'll run up a fine bill for extra time, but, after all, it's less extravagant than a good many other things. Wonder how much they charge for overtime. I must ask Daddy."

With a smile of anticipation Patty picked up the telephone.

"Hello!" said Mr. Cameron's eager voice. "I thought you'd never come. I've been waiting since ten."

"I've been to the opera," said Patty, nonchalantly. "And you've NO reason to sit and wait for me! I'm not a dead certainty, like the sunrise or the postman."

"You're more welcome than either."

"Now that's a real pretty speech. Are you a poet?"

"Only to you."

"Did you get the pictures?" Patty was unable longer to restrain her impatience.

"Of course I got the pictures. I knew yours at once! You needn't think you can fool ME."

"Which was mine? The girl with the black curls?"

"Mercy, no! I know you're not THAT type. She looks like an actress, and hasn't a brain in her silly head. And you're not that lackadaisical lily-like one, either. Oh, I know YOU! You're that delightful, sensible, really brainy girl with the smooth black hair."

"Oh, I AM, am I?"

"Yes; and I'm SO glad you're not a rattle-pated beauty! What's a pretty face compared to real mind and intellect!"

Patty was furious. She didn't aspire to nor desire this great mind and intellect, and she was quite satisfied with the amount of brains in her pretty, curly head.

"I don't think much of your taste!" she exclaimed.

"Why! you don't want me to be disappointed because you're not pretty, do you?"

"But I AM pretty."

"Yes; as I said, the beauty of deep thought and education shines from your clear eyes. That is far better than dimples and curls."

Patty shook her curls at the telephone and her dimples came and went with her varying emotions.

"Why, I shouldn't like you half as well if you were pretty," Mr. Cameron went on. "The only things I consider worth while are seriousness and scholarship. These you have in abundance, as I can see at once from your picture."

"And how do you like the way I dress?"

"It suits your type exactly. That large black-and-white check denotes a mind far above the frivolities of fashion, and that stiff white collar, to my mind, indicates a high order of mentality."

"I think you're perfectly horrid!" And this exclamation seemed wrung from the depths of Patty's soul.

A ringing laugh answered her - a laugh so hearty and so full of absolute enjoyment that Patty listened in astonishment.

"Poor little Princess Poppycheek! It's a shame to tease her! WAS she maligned by a bad, horrid man that she doesn't even know? There, Little Girl, don't cry! I know perfectly well that stiff old schoolmarm isn't you! Now, will you tell me who you are, and what you really look like?"

Patty had to think quickly. She had supposed that Cameron meant what he said, but after all he was fooling her. And she had thought she fooled him!

"Which is me, then?" she said, in a small, low voice.

"None of 'em! You goosie! To think you could fool ME. In the first place, I knew you wouldn't send your own photograph; and when I saw those three charming specimens, in out-of-date clothes, I knew you had ransacked your album to find them. However, I took the whole bunch down to Marie, and she vowed she had never laid eyes on one of them before. So there, now!"

"Then we're just back where we started from," said Patty, cheerfully.

"Yes; but, if you'll come to the musicale on Friday night, we can make great progress in a short time."

"I told you I'd go, if you would persuade Marie to invite me."

"Nonsense! I believe she HAS invited you. I believe you're Miss Curtiss. SHE has dark hair."

"Why not that other singer, Miss Fairfield?"

"Oh, Marie says she's a blonde. The 'raving beauty' sort. I detest that kind. I know she's vain."

"Yes, she is. I hate to speak against another girl, but I know that Patty Fairfield, and she IS vain."

"Well, never mind about Patty Fairfield She doesn't interest me a bit. But what about you? Will you come to the party? Oh, DO-ee, DO-ee, - now, - as my old Scotch nurse used to say. Come to your waiting knight!"

Kit's voice was very wheedlesome, and Patty was

moved to encourage him a little.

"Do you know, - I almost think - that maybe - possibly - perhaps, I WILL go."

"Really? Oh, Poppycheek, I'm SO glad! I do want to see My Girl!"

"YOUR girl, indeed!"

"Yes; mine by right of discovery."

"But you haven't discovered me yet."

"But I will, - on Friday night. You'll TRULY come, WON'T you?"

"Honest, I've never been where I wasn't invited -"

"But this is different -"

"Yes, - it IS different -"

"Oh, then you will come! Goody, GOODY! I'm so glad!"

"Don't break the telephone with your gladness! Suppose I DO come, how will you know me? How will you know that it is I?"

"Oh, I'll know! 'I shall know it, I shall feel it, something subtle will reveal it, for a glory round thee hovers that will lighten up the gloom.'"

"Oh, you ARE a poet."

"I am a poet, but I didn't write that. However, it was only because the other fellow got ahead of me."

"Who was he? Who wrote it?"

"I'll tell you Friday night. Come early, won't you?"
"No; I always get to a party late."

"Don't be too late. I want to play to you. And will you sing?"

"Mercy, gracious! I might go to a party without being invited, but I can't SING without being asked. You tell Marie I'm coming, will you?"

"You bet I will. What shall you wear?"

"What's your favourite colour?"

"Red."

"Red is becoming to brunettes; but I haven't any red evening gown. How about yellow?"

"All right, wear yellow. I shall adore you in any colour."

"Well; perhaps I'll come, and perhaps I won't. Good-night."

Patty hung up the receiver with a sudden click, and Mr. Kit Cameron was left very much in doubt as to whether the whole thing was a joke or not.

CHAPTER VI

PRINCESS POPPYCHEEK

On the night of the musicale at Marie Homer's, her talented cousin arrived long before any guests were expected.

"I couldn't wait, Aunt Frances," he said, as Mrs. Homer greeted him. "I'm so impatient to see My Girl."

Kit had told the Homers of the telephone conversations, because he was so anxious to find out his lady's name. Of course, he had not told all they said, and from his incoherent ravings about a black-haired beauty Marie never guessed he could mean Patty.

"You're a foolish boy, Kit," said his Aunt.

"I don't believe that girl is any one we know, but is some mischievous hoyden who is leading you a dance. You won't see her to-night, - if you ever do."

"Then I shall think up the easiest death possible, and die it," declared Kit, cheerfully. "Why, you know, Aunt Frances, I never took any interest in a girl before, except of course Marie and Bee, but this girl is so different from everybody else in the world. Her voice is like a chime of silver bells, - and her laugh -"

"There, there, Kit, I haven't time to listen to your rhapsodies! You're here altogether too early, and you'll have to excuse me, for I have some household matters to look after. Marie isn't quite dressed yet, so you'll have to amuse yourself for awhile. Play some sentimental music on your violin, if that fits your mood."

With a kindly smile at her nephew, Mrs. Homer bustled away, and Kit was left alone in the music-room.

He played some soft, low music for a time, and then Marie came in.

"You're an old goose, Kit," she remarked, affectionately, "to think that mysterious girl of yours will be here to-night. There isn't anybody who knows me well enough to come without an invitation, that I haven't already invited. I've added to my list of invitations until it now numbers about thirty, and that's all the really musical friends I have. If this girl of yours sings as well as you say, she's probably a soubrette or a chorus girl."

"Nothing of the sort!" Kit exclaimed. "She's the sweetest, daintiest, refinedest, culturedest little thing you ever saw!"

"How do you know? You haven't seen her."

"No, but I've talked with her. I guess I know." And Kit turned decidedly sulky, for he began to think it WAS rather doubtful about his seeing his girl that evening.

And then the guests began to arrive, and Mr. Kit put on

a smiling face and made himself agreeable to his cousin's friends.

Patty came among the latest arrivals. She looked her prettiest in a filmy gown of pale-blue chiffon, with touches of silver embroidery. An ornament in her hair was of silver filigree, with a wisp of pale-blue feather, and her cheeks were a little pinker than usual.

Kit glanced at her as she came in, and, though he noticed that she was an extremely pretty girl, he immediately glanced away again and continued his watch for the black-eyed girl he expected. The room was well filled by this time, and Patty took a seat near the front, where sat a group of her intimate friends. They greeted her gaily, and Kit, on the other side of the room, paid no attention to them.

The programme began with a duet by Kit on his violin, and his Cousin Marie at the piano.

The man was really a virtuoso, and his beautiful playing held the audience spellbound. Patty watched him, enthralled with his music, and admiring, too, his generally worth-while appearance.

"He does look awfully jolly," she thought, to herself, "and it's plain to be seen he has brains. I wonder if he will be terribly disappointed in me, after all. I've a notion to run away."

For the first time in her life Patty felt shy about singing. Usually she had no trace of self-consciousness, but to-night she experienced a feeling of embarrassment she had never known before. She realized this, and scolded herself roundly for it. "You idiot!"

she observed, mentally, to her own soul; "if you want to make a good impression, you'd better stop feeling like a simpleton. Now brace up, and do the best you can, and behave yourself!"

Miss Curtiss sang before Patty did. She was a sweet-faced young woman, with a beautiful and well-trained contralto voice. Patty cast a furtive glance at Kit Cameron, and found that he was looking intently at the singer. She knew perfectly well he was wondering whether this might be the girl of the telephone conversations, and she saw, too, that he decided in the negative, for he shook his head slightly, but with conviction.

Suddenly the humour of the whole situation struck Patty. The incident was not serious, but humorous, and as soon as she realised this her shyness disappeared, and the spirit of mischief once again took possession of her. She knew now she would do herself credit when she sang, and when her turn came she rose and walked slowly and gracefully to the platform which had been temporarily placed for the musicians.

Marie was to play her accompaniment, and Patty had expected to sing first a somewhat elaborate aria, using "Beware" as an encore.

But as she reached the platform, and as she noticed Kit Cameron's face, its expression politely interested, but in no wise enthusiastic, she suddenly changed her mind. She put the music of "Beware" on the piano rack, and murmured to Marie, "This one first."

Marie looked puzzled, but of course she couldn't say anything as Patty stood waiting to begin.

For some reason Patty was always at her prettiest when she sang. She thoroughly enjoyed singing, and she enjoyed the evident pleasure it gave to others. She stood gracefully, her hands lightly clasped before her, and the added excitement of this particular occasion gave a flush to her cheek and a sparkle to her blue eyes that made her positively bewitching.

And then she sang the foolish little song, "Beware," just as she had sung it over the telephone, coquettishly, but without artificiality or forced effect.

She scarcely dared look at Kit Cameron. A fleeting glance showed her that he was probably at that moment the most nonplussed young man in existence.

She looked away quickly, lest her voice should falter from amusement.

Luckily, all the audience were regarding Patty attentively, and had no eyes for the astonished face of Kit Cameron. He had taken no special interest in the blonde singer, but when her first notes, rang out he started in surprise. As the voice continued he knew at once it was the same voice he had heard over the telephone, but he couldn't reconcile the facts. He caught the fleeting glance she gave him, he saw the roguish smile in her eyes, and he was forced to believe that this girl was his dark-eyed unknown.

"The little rascal!" he said, to himself. "The scamp! the rogue! How she has tricked me! To think she was Patty Fairfield all the time! No wonder Marie didn't know whom I was talking about! Well!"

As the song finished no one applauded more

enthusiastically than Kit Cameron.

But Patty would not look toward him, and proceeded to sing as an encore the aria she had intended to sing first.

She was in her best voice, and she sang this beautifully, and, if the audience was surprised at the unusual order of the selections, they were unstinted in their applause.

Leaving the stage, instead of returning to her seat, Patty stepped back into the next room, which was the library.

Cameron was there to receive her. He had felt sure she would not return to the audience immediately, and he took the chance.

He held out both hands and Patty laid her hands in his.

"Captive Princess," he murmured.

"My Knight!" Patty whispered, and flashed a smile at him.

"Can you EVER forgive the things I said?" he asked, earnestly, as he led her across the room and they sat down on a divan.

"There's nothing to forgive," she said, smiling; "you detest blondes, I know, but I'm thinking seriously of dyeing my hair black."

"Don't! that would be a sacrilege! And you MUST remember that I told you I always adored blondes, until you told me you were brunette."

"But I didn't," said Patty, laughing. "Somehow you got the notion that I was dark, and I didn't correct it. Are you TERRIBLY disappointed in me?"

Naughty Patty raised her heavenly blue eyes and looked so like a fair, sweet flower that Kit exclaimed:

"Disappointed! You are an angel, straight from heaven!"

"Nonsense! If you talk like that, I shall run away."

"Don't run away! I'll talk any way you like, but now that I have found you I shall keep you. But I am still in depths of self-abasement. Didn't I say most unkind things about Miss Fairfield?"

"No unkinder than I did. We both jumped on her, and said she was vain and horrid."

"*I* never said such dreadful things! I'm sure I didn't. But, if I did, I shall spend the rest of my life making up for it. And I called you Poppycheek!"

Cameron looked at Patty's cheeks in such utter dismay that she laughed outright.

"But you know," she said, "there are pink poppies as well as scarlet. Incidentally there are white and there are saffron yellow."

"So there are," said Cameron, delightedly. "How you DO help a fellow out! Well, yours are just the colour of a soft , dainty pink poppy that is touched by the sunlight and kissed by a summer breeze."

"I knew you were a poet," said Patty, smiling, "but I don't allow even a summer breeze to kiss my cheeks."

"I should hope not! A summer breeze is altogether too promiscuous with its kisses. I hope you don't allow any kisses, except those of your own particular swansdown powder puff."

"Of course I don't!" laughed Patty, and then she blushed furiously as she suddenly remembered how Farnsworth had kissed both her cheeks the night of Christine's wedding.

"I see you're blushing at a memory," said Cameron, coolly; "I suppose the powder puff was too audacious."

"Yes, that's it," said Patty, her liking for this young man increased by the pleasantry of his light banter. "And now we must return to the music-room. I came here a moment to catch my breath after singing; but how did you happen to be here?"

"I knew you'd come here; ostensibly, of course, to catch your breath, but really because you knew I'd be here."

"You wretch!" cried Patty. "How dare you say such things! I never dreamed you'd be here; if I had, I shouldn't have come."

"Of course you wouldn't, you little coquette! It's your nature to be perverse and capricious. But your sweet good-humour won't let you carry those other traits too far. Oh, I know you, My Girl!"

Carolyn Wells

"I object to that phrase from you," Patty said, coldly, "and I must ask you not to use it again."

"But you ARE my girl, by right of discovery. By the way, you're not anybody else's girl, are you?"

"Just what do you mean by that?"

"Well, in other words, then, are you engaged, betrothed, plighted, promised, bespoke -"

Patty burst out laughing. "I'm not any of those things," she said, "but, if ever I am, I shall be bespoke. I think that's the loveliest word! Fancy being anybody's Bespoke!"

"Of course, it's up to me to give you an immediate opportunity," said Cameron, sighing. "But somehow I don't quite dare bespeak you on such short acquaintance."

"Faint heart -"

"Oh, it isn't that! I'm brave enough. But I'm an awfully punctilious man. If I were going to bespeak you, now, I should think it my duty to go first to your father and correctly ask his permission to pay my addresses to his daughter."

"Good gracious! How do you pay addresses? I never had an address paid to me in my life."

"Shall I show you how?" And Cameron jumped up and fell on one knee before Patty, with a comical expression of a make-believe love-sick swain.

Patty dearly loved fooling, and she smiled back at him roguishly, and just at that moment Philip Van Reypen came into the room.

In the dim half-light he descried Patty on the divan and Cameron kneeling before her, and, as Mr. Van Reypen was blessed with a quick temper, he felt a sudden desire to choke the talented Mr. Cameron.

"Patty!" Philip exclaimed, angrily.

"Yes, Philip," said Patty, in a voice of sweet humility.

"Come with me," was the stern command.

"Yes, Philip," and Patty arose and walked away with Van Reypen, leaving Kit Cameron still on his knee.

"Well, I'll be hammered!" that gentleman remarked, as he rose slowly and deliberately dusted off his knee with his handkerchief; "that girl is a wonder! She's full of the dickens, but she's as sweet as a peach. I always did like blondes best, whether she believes it or not. But if I hadn't, I should now. There's only one girl in the world for me. I wonder if she is mixed up with that Van Reypen chap. He had a most proprietary manner, but all the same, that little witch is quite capable of scooting off like that, just to tease me. Oh, I'll play her own game and meet her on her own ground. Little Poppycheek!" With a nonchalant air, Mr. Cameron sauntered back to the music-room, and seated himself beside Miss Curtiss, with whom he struck up an animated conversation, not so much as glancing at Patty.

Patty observed this from the corner of her eye, and she

nodded her head in approval.

"He's worth knowing," she thought; "I'll have a lot of fun with him."

The programme was almost over, but Kit was to play once again. With Marie, he played a fine selection, and then, as he was tumultuously encored, he went back to the platform alone. Without accompaniment he played the little song, "Beware," that Patty had sung, and, improvising, he made a fantasia of the air. He was clever as well as skilled, and he turned the simple little melody into thrilling, rollicking music with trills and roulades until the original theme was almost lost sight of, only to crop up again with new intensity.

Patty listened, enthralled. She loved this sort of thing, and she knew he was playing to her and for her. The strains would be now softly romantic, now grandly triumphant, but ever recurring to the main motive, until one seemed fairly to see the fickle maiden of the song.

When it was ended, the room rang with applause. Cameron bowed simply, and laying aside his violin, went straight to Patty and sat down by her, coolly appropriating the chair which his cousin Marie had just left.

"I made that for you," he said, simply. "Did you like it?"

"Like it!" exclaimed Patty, her blue eyes dancing; "I revelled in it! It was wonderful! Was it really impromptu?"

"Of course. It was nothing. Any one can play

variations on an old song."

"Variations nothing!" remarked Patty. "It was a work, - a chef d'oeuvre, - an opus!"

"Yes; Opus One of my new cycle." "What are you two talking about?" said Marie, returning. "Have you found your girl, Kit? What do you think, Patty? - Kit's crazy over a black-eyed girl whom he doesn't know!"

"Is he?" said Patty, dropping her eyes demurely.

"I found My Girl, Marie," Cameron announced, calmly; "I find I made a trifling mistake about her colouring, but that's a mere detail. As it turns out, the lady of my quest is Miss Fairfield."

"Good gracious, are you, Patty?" said Marie, impetuously; "are you Kit's girl?"

"Yes; I am," and Patty folded her hands with a ridiculous air of complacency.

"Patty!" growled Van Reypen, who was sitting behind her.

"Yes, Philip," said Patty, sweetly, turning partly round.

"Behave yourself!"

"I am behaving, Philip," and Patty looked very meek.

"Of course you are," said Marie; "you're behaving beautifully. And you look like an angel, and you sang like a lark, and if you're Kit's Girl, I'm glad of it. Now come on, everybody's going to supper."

"You come along with me," said Philip Van Reypen, as he took Patty by the arm.

"Why?" And Patty looked a little defiant at this command.

"Because I want you to. And I want you to stop making up to that Cameron man."

"I'm not, Philip; he's making up to me."

"Well, he'd better stop it! What was he doing on his knees before you in the library?"

"I don't remember," said Patty, innocently. "Oh, yes, he was telling me my cheeks were red, or some foolishness like that."

"And your eyes were blue, I suppose, and your hair was yellow! Didn't you know all those things before?"

"Why, Philip, how cross you are! Yes, I've known those things for nineteen years. It's no surprise to me."

"Patty, I'd like to shake you! Do you know what you are? You're just a little, vain, silly, babbling coquette!"

"I think that's a lovely thing to be! Do you want me to babble to you, Philip, or shall I go and babble to somebody else?"

"Don't babble at all. Here's a chair. You sit right down here, and eat your supper. Here's another chair. You lay your shawl and bonnet on that, to keep it for me, and I'll go and forage for some food."

Patty laid her scarf and fan on the chair to reserve it for Philip, but she was not unduly surprised when Mr. Cameron came along, picked up her belongings, and seated himself in the chair.

"That's Mr. Van Reypen's chair," said Patty; "if he finds you there, he'll gently but firmly kill you."

"I know it," said Kit, placidly; "but a Knight is always willing to brave death for his Lady."

"But I don't want you killed," said Patty, looking sad, "I wouldn't have anybody to telephone to."

"If I run away then, to save my life, will you telephone me to-night?"

"Indeed I won't! that's all over. But please, Mr. Cameron, run away, for here comes Philip, with both hands full of soup, and I know he wouldn't hesitate to scald you with it."

Mr. Cameron arose, as Mr. Van Reypen came in, and with an air of willingly relinquishing his seat to Philip, he said, "My Girl's Orders."

Philip didn't hear it, but Patty did, and she blushed, for Cameron's departure that way showed greater deference to her wishes than if he had stayed with her.

"What did he say?" Philip asked, as he offered Patty a cup of bouillon, and then sat down beside her.

"He said you were such a sweet-tempered man, he didn't wonder I liked you," and Patty beamed pleasantly.

"I would be sweet-tempered, Patty, if you didn't tease the very life out of me!"

"Now, Philip, you wouldn't be much good if you couldn't stand a little teasing."

"Go ahead, then; tease me all you like," and Van Reypen looked the personification of dogged endurance.

"I will!" said Patty, emphatically, and then some others joined them, and the group began to laugh and talk together.

"Your cousin is stunning, Marie," said Mona Galbraith; "why have we never met him before?"

"He's a freak," Marie said, laughingly. "I couldn't persuade him to come to my valentine party, and to-night I couldn't keep him away! All musicians are freaks, you know."

"He's a musician, all right," said Kenneth Harper. "The things he did to that simple little song must have made some of the eminent composers turn in their graves!"

"He's awfully clever at that sort of thing," said Marie; "sometimes when we're here alone, he'll take a simple little air and improvise the most beautiful melodies from it."

"Is he amiable?" asked Mona, casually.

"Not very; or rather, not always. But he's a dear fellow, and we're all fond of him. How did you like him, Patty?"

"I thought he was lovely," said Patty, and Van Reypen glared at her.

CHAPTER VII

SUITORS

After supper the whole party went to the large drawing-room to dance.

Kit Cameron made a bee-line for Patty. "You'll give me the first dance, won't you?" he said, simply, "because I've stayed away from you all supper time."

Patty hesitated. "I'm willing, Mr. Cameron," she said, "but for one thing. I'm awfully exacting in the matter of dancing, and if you're not a good dancer it would go far to spoil our pleasant acquaintance. Suppose we don't risk it."

Cameron considered. "I am a good dancer," he said, "but Marie has told me that you're something phenomenal in that line. So I daresay you will be disappointed in me. All right, suppose we don't risk it."

Cameron half turned away, as if he had relinquished the idea of dancing with Patty, and that young woman was somewhat taken aback. She had assumed her new friend would insist on dancing with her, and she had no mind to let him escape thus. She was just about to say, impulsively, "Oh well, let's try it, anyway," when she caught a gleam from the corner of his eye, and she realised in a flash that he felt sure she would call him back!

This was enough for capricious Patty, and she turned away from him, but not so quickly but that she saw his face suddenly fall, proving that she had been quite right in her diagnosis of the case.

She smiled on Van Reypen, who was hovering near, and he came to her at once.

"Our dance, Patty?" he said, eagerly, holding out his hand.

"Yes, Philip," she answered simply, laying her hand in his. and in a moment they were circling the room.

"Don't be cross to me, will you, Philip?" said Patty with an appealing note in her soft voice.

"No; you little torment, you. I'll never be cross to you, if you won't flirt with other men."

"Philip," and Patty spoke quite seriously, "I'll be cross with you, if you don't stop taking that attitude with me. It isn't for YOU to say whether I shall flirt with other men or not!"

"No, I know it;" and Philip was unexpectedly humble. "I wish it was for me to say, Patty."

"Stop talking nonsense, or I'll stop dancing with you! By the way, Phil, you're an awfully good dancer."

"I'm glad there's something about me that pleases your ladyship."

"Yes; so am I. It certainly isn't your temper!"

And then Philip smiled into Patty's eyes, and peace was restored, as it always was after their little squabbles.

The dance over, they sat for a few moments, and then Kenneth Harper asked to be Patty's next partner.

"All right, Ken," said Patty; "but sit down here just a minute; I want to watch the others."

What Patty really wanted was to see Mr. Cameron dance; and in a few moments he went past them with Elise.

"That man's all round clever," commented Kenneth. "He dances just as he plays the violin, exquisitely. Why, Patty, he's a poem in patent leathers!"

Sure enough, Kit Cameron was an unusually fine dancer, and Patty felt a slow blush rising to her cheeks, as she remembered what she had said to him, and realised he must have thought her vain of her dancing.

For once, Patty felt honestly ashamed of herself. She had implied that she was such a fine dancer she didn't care to dance with any one unskilled in the art.

But after all, this was not quite Patty's attitude. When a stranger was introduced to her, she was quite willing to dance with him, whether he danced well or not. But as to Mr. Cameron, Patty liked him so much and so enjoyed his beautiful music, that she really felt it would be a shock to their friendship if he danced awkwardly.

And, too, she never for a moment supposed he would take her at her word. She had supposed he would insist upon the dance, even after her hesitation.

"What's the matter Patty?" said Kenneth; "you look as though you'd lost your last friend!"

"I'm not sure but I have," said Patty, smiling a little. For certainly Mr. Cameron was the last friend she had made, and it was very likely that she had lost him.

"Well, never mind, you still have me left. I'm gentle and I'm kind, and you'll never, never find a better friend than your old Ken."

"I believe you're right," and Patty smiled at him. "We've been friends a long time, haven't we, Ken?"

"We sure have. When I look at your gray hair and wrinkled cheeks, I realise that we are growing old together."

Patty laughed and dimpled at this nonsense, and then declared she was ready to dance.

All through the evening, Patty was gaily whisked from one partner to another, but Kit Cameron never came near her.

She was decidedly chagrined at this, even though she knew she had only herself to blame for it. She had been really rude, and she was reaping the well-deserved consequences.

Often she passed Cameron in the dance, as he whirled by with another girl. He always smiled pleasantly as they passed, and the fact that he was a magnificent dancer only made Patty feel more angry with herself at having been so silly.

Just before the last dance, Patty stood, gaily chatting with several of her friends, when the music struck up, and both Kenneth and Philip claimed the dance.

"You promised it to me, Patty," said Kenneth, reproachfully.

"Why, Ken Harper, I didn't do any such thing!" and Patty's big blue eyes gazed at him in honest surprise.

"Of course you didn't, you promised it to me," said Van Reypen, equally mendacious.

"Why, I didn't promise it to anybody!" declared Patty; "I haven't promised a dance ahead this whole evening."

As she stood, with the two insistent applicants on either side of her, Cameron walked straight toward her. He said not a word, but held out his arm, and calmly walking away from her two disappointed suitors, Patty was at once whirled away.

"Well, Princess Poppycheek, - Princess Pink Poppycheek, - I had to surrender," Cameron said, as they floated around the room. "After your cruel aspersion on my dancing, I was so enraged I vowed to myself I'd never speak to you again. But I'm awful magnanimous, and I forgive you freely, from the bottom of my heart."

"I haven't asked to be forgiven," and Patty shot him a saucy glance; "but," she added, shyly, "I'm truly glad you do forgive me. I was a pig!"

"So you were. A Poppycheeked piggy-wig! But with me, what is forgiven is forgotten. And, by the way, you dance fairly well."

"So I've been told," returned Patty, demurely. "And I find I can get along with you."

This sounded like faint praise, but each knew that the other appreciated how well their steps suited each other and how skilful they both were.

Van Reypen and Ken Harper stood where Patty had left them, for a moment, as they watched their hoped-for partner dance away.

"There's no use getting mad at that child," said Ken, patiently; "she WILL do as she likes."

"Well, after all, why shouldn't she? She's a reigning belle, and she's a law unto herself. But she has a lot of sense inside that golden curly head."

"Yes," returned Kenneth, "and not only sense, but a sound, sweet nature. Patty is growing up a coquette, but it is only because she is beset by flattery; and, too, she IS full of mischief. She can't help teasing her suitors, as she calls them."

"She can tease me all she likes," said Van Reypen, somewhat seriously, and Kenneth answered simply, "Me, too."

Next morning, Patty told Nan all about Mr. Cameron, and that gay little lady was greatly interested in the story.

"I knew he would be nice," said Nan, "from what you had already told me about him. Is he good-looking, Patty?"

"Yes, - no, - I don't know," returned Patty; "I don't believe I thought about it. He has an awfully nice face, and he's tall and big, and yet he's young-looking. At least, his eyes are. He has dark eyes, and they're just brimming over with mischief and fun, except when he's playing his violin."

"Then I suppose he has the regulation 'far away' look," commented Nan.

"Well, he doesn't look like a dying goat, if that's what you mean! but he looks like a real musician, and he is one."

"And a woman-hater, I believe?"

"Oh, it's rubbish to call him that! He's not crazy over girls, but it's because he thinks most of them are silly. He likes his two cousins, - and, Nan, don't breathe it, but I have a faint inkling of a suspicion of a premonition that he's going to like me!"

"Patty, you're a conceited little goose!"

"Nay, nay, my ducky stepmother, but I'd be a poor stick if I couldn't fascinate that youth after our romantic introduction."

"That's so; and I think you'll not have much trouble bringing him to your feet."

"Oh, I don't want him at my feet. And I don't want him

to fall in love with me. I hate that sort of thing! I want him for a nice, chummy, comrade friend, and if I can't have him that way, I don't want him at all. There's Philip and Kenneth now; they've always been so nice. But lately they've taken to making sheep's eyes at me and flinging out bits of foolishness here and there that make me tired! A debutante's life is not a happy one!"

Patty drew such a long, deep sigh, that Nan burst into laughter.

"I would feel sorry for you, Patty," she said, "but I can't help thinking that you're quite able to look out for yourself."

"'Deed I am! When they talk mush, I just giggle at 'em. It brings 'em down pretty quick from their highfalutin nonsense!"

The two were sitting in Patty's boudoir, which was such a bright, sunny room that many a morning hour was pleasantly passed together there by these two friends. Patty was fortunate in having a stepmother so in sympathy with her pursuits and pleasures, and Nan was equally fortunate in having warm-hearted, sunny-natured Patty with her.

Jane came in, bringing an enormous box from a florist.

"My prophetic soul!" cried Patty. "My efforts were not in vain! I feel it in my funnybone that my latest Prince Charming has sent me a posy."

Nor was she wrong. The box contained a bewildering array of spring flowers. Delicate blossoms of jonquils, hyacinths , lilacs, daffodils, and other dainty, fragile flowers that breathed of spring.

"Aren't they lovely!" And Patty buried her face in the fragrant mass of bloom.

"Here's a card," said Nan, picking up a white envelope.

Patty drew out Mr. Cameron's card, and on it was written: "To Princess Poppycheek; that they may tell all that I may not speak."

"Now that's a real nice sentiment," Patty declared; "you see, it doesn't commit him to anything, and yet it sounds pretty. Oh, I shall end by adoring that young man! Bring me some bowls and things, please, Jane; I want to arrange this flower garden myself."

Jane departed with the box and papers, and returned with a tray, on which were several bowls and vases filled with water.

Patty always enjoyed arranging flowers, and she massed them in the bowls, with taste and skill as to color and arrangement.

"There!" she said, as she finished her task; "they do look beautiful, though I say it as shouldn't. Now, I think I shall sit me down and write a sweet gushing note of thanks, while I'm in the notion. For I've a lot on to-day, and I can't devote much time to this particular suitor."

"Suitor is a slang word, Patty; you oughtn't to use it."

"Fiddle-dee-dee! if I didn't use any slang, I couldn't talk at all! And suitor isn't exactly slang; it's the word in current fashion for any pleasant young gentleman who sends flowers, or otherwise favors any pleasant young lady. Everybody in society knows what it means, so don't act old fogy, - Nancy Dancy."

Patty dropped a butterfly kiss on Nan's brow, and then pirouetted across the room to her writing desk.

"Shall I begin, 'My Dear Suitor'?" she said, and then giggled to see the shocked look on Nan's face.

"It wouldn't matter; he would understand," she said, carelessly, "but I think I can do better than that."

"Well, I'll leave you to yourself," said Nan; "not out of special consideration for your comfort, but because it doesn't interest me to watch anybody write letters."

"By-by," and Patty waved her hand, absentmindedly, as Nan left the room.

Then she applied herself to her task.

"Most Courteous Knight," she began; "The flowers are beautiful, - and they are saying lovely things to me. They say they are fresh and young and green. Oh, my goodness! I forgot that you said they were speaking for you! Well, then, they are saying that they are just the sort I like, and they are sure of a welcome. With many, many thanks, I am very sincerely yours, Patricia Poppycheek Fairfield."

And then Patty dismissed her Knight from her mind, and turned her attention to other matters. That afternoon about five o'clock, Mr. Cameron called.

"I scarcely hoped to find you at home," he said, as Patty greeted him in the drawing-room.

"It isn't our day," she returned, "but I chanced to be in, and I'm glad of it. Nan, may I present Mr. Cameron?" And Nan accorded a pleasant welcome to the visitor.

"You see, Mrs. Fairfield," Cameron said, "I rarely go into society and I fear my manners are a bit rusty. So if I have come to call too soon, please forgive me."

His smile was so frank and his manner so easily correct, that Nan approved of him at once. She was punctilious in such matters, and she saw, through Kit's pretence at rustiness, that he was not lacking in etiquette or courtesy.

"Let's have tea in the library," said Patty; "you see, Mr. Cameron, we always invite people we like to have tea in there, rather than in this formal place."

"That suits me; I want to be considered one of the family, and what's the use of wasting a whole lot of time getting up to that point? Let's make believe we've always known each other."

So tea was served in the library, and a very pleasant informal feast it was.

Mr. Fairfield came in, and soon the whole quartette were chatting gaily as if they had always known each other.

Mr. Cameron was especially interested in Patty's club called "Happy Saturdays."

"It's the kindest thing I ever heard of," he said, enthusiastically. "It does good to people who can't be reached by any organised charity. I don't want to intrude, Miss Fairfield, and I don't want to exploit myself, but if you ever give your Saturday friends a little musicale or anything like that, I'd jolly well like to play for you. I'll play popular stuff, or I'll play my best Sunday-go-to-meeting pieces, whichever you prefer."

"That's awfully nice of you," said Patty, smiling at him. "I've often thought I'd get up something of that sort."

"We might have it here," said Nan, "unless you mean to invite more people than we could take care of."

"I'd like to have it here," said Patty; "the drawing-room would easily seat sixty or seventy in an audience, - perhaps more. And I don't believe we could find more than that to invite. Although I know of a girls' club that I'd like to invite as a whole."

"It's a pretty big thing you're getting up, Pattikins," said Mr. Fairfield, smiling kindly at his enthusiastic daughter, "but if you think you can swing it, go ahead. I'll help all I can."

"It would upset the house terribly," said Nan; "but I don't mind that. I'm with you, Patty. Let's do it."

"If you're shy on the programme, I can get one or two fellows to help us out," said Cameron. "A chum of mine warbles a good baritone and I'm dead sure he'd like to help."

"I'm really a perfectly good singer," said Mr. Fairfield, "but my voice is not appreciated nowadays. So I'm going to decline all requests to sing, however insistent. But I'll help you out this way, Patsy-Poppet. I'll set up the supper for the whole crowd."

"Oh, daddy, how good you are!" and Patty leaned over to give her father's hand an affectionate squeeze. "It will be just lovely! We'll give those people a real musical treat, and a lovely supper to wind up with. Really, Mr. Cameron, you are to be thanked for all this, for you first suggested it. Our club has never done such a big thing before. I know the girls will be delighted!"

Unable to wait, Patty flew to the telephone and called up Mona, who was one of the most earnest workers of the club. As she had fore-seen, Mona was greatly pleased, and they immediately planned a meeting for the next morning to perfect the arrangements.

"And incidentally, and aside from giving a musical entertainment to your poor but worthy young friends, won't you go with me next week to enjoy some music yourself?" said Cameron to Patty, as he was about to take leave.

"Where?" she asked.

"I want to have a little opera party. Only half a dozen of us. The Hepworths will be our chaperons, and if you will go, I'll ask my cousin Marie and Mr. Harper."

"Why not Mr. Van Reypen?" said Patty, mischievously.

"Me deadly rival! never! nevaire! how could you cruelly suggest it?"

"I didn't mean it. Forget it," and Patty smiled at him.

"All right, it's forgotten, but don't EVER let such a thing occur again!"

And then Mr. Cameron reluctantly took himself off.

Carolyn Wells

CHAPTER VIII

A HOUSE PARTY

Somehow or other Mr. Cameron immediately became a prominent factor in the Fairfield household. He appeared frequently, and even more frequently he telephoned or he wrote notes or he sent flowers or messages, until Patty declared he was everlastingly under foot!

But he was so gay and good-natured, so full of pranks and foolery, that it was impossible to snub him or to be annoyed with him.

He was a civil engineer, having already built up a good-sized business. But he seemed to be both able and willing to leave his office at any hour of the day or night for any occasion where Patty was concerned.

But he apparently fulfilled her wishes as to being her friend and chum and comrade, without falling in love with her.

"He's a thoroughly nice chap," Mr. Fairfield often said; "good-natured and right-minded, as well as clever and talented."

So, as he was also a favourite with Nan, he dropped in

at the Fairfield house very often, and Patty grew to like him very much.

The opera party had duly taken place and had been a pleasant success. The musical entertainment was being planned for some weeks hence, as it was not easy to find a near-by date which suited all concerned.

One morning, as Patty was fluttering around her boudoir and looking over her mail, the telephone rang and the familiar "Hello, Princess," sounded in her ear.

"Hello, most noble Knight," she responded, "what would'st thou of me?"

"A boon so great that I fear to ask it! Won't you promise it in advance?"

"What I promise in advance, I never fulfil."

"Don't do it, then! I'll ask you first. You see, it's this way. My angelic and altogether delightful sister Lora lives in Eastchester with her stalwart husband and a blossom-bud of a kiddy. Now it seems that there's a wonderful country-club ball up there, and she thinks it will be nice if you and I should attend that same."

"And what do YOU think about it?"

"Oh, I don't have any thoughts concerning it, until I know what YOU think. And then, of course, that's precisely what *I* think."

"When is it?"

"To-morrow night."

"Mercy me! So soon! Well, I haven't anything on for to-morrow night; but the next night Mr. Van Reypen is making a theatre party for me that I wouldn't miss for anything."

"H'm! how LOVELY! Well, Princess, what say you to my humble plea?"

"What are your plans? How do I get there?"

"Why, thusly; my sister will invite you to her home, and incidentally to the ball. She will also ask my cousin Marie and Mr. Harper, who is not at all averse, it seems to me, to playing Marie's little lamb!"

"Have you noticed that? So have I. Well, go on."

"Well, then, I thought it would be nice if we four should motor out to Eastchester to-morrow afternoon, go straight to sister's, do up the ball business and motor back the next day. There's the whole case in a nutshell. Now pronounce my doom!"

"It seems to me just the nicest sort of a racket, and if your sister invites me, I shall most certainly accept."

"Oh, bless you for ever! Princess Poppycheek. I shall telephone Lora at once, and she will write you an invitation on her best stationery, and she will also telephone you, and if you wish it she will come and call on you."

"No, don't bother her to do that. I've met her, you know, and if she either writes or telephones, it will be all right. What time do we start?"

"About three, so as to make it easily by tea-time."

"I'll be ready. Count on me. Good-bye."

Patty hung up the telephone suddenly, as she always did. She often said it was her opinion that more time was wasted in this world by people who didn't know how to say good-bye, than from any other cause. And her minutes were too precious to be spent on a telephone, after the main subject of conversation had been finished.

She danced downstairs to tell Nan all about it.

"Very nice party," Nan approved; "I've met Mrs. Perry, you know, and she's charming. You'll be home Thursday, of course. You know you've a theatre party that night."

"Yes, I know; I'll be home," said Patty, abstractedly. "What would you take for the ball, Nan? My pink chiffon or my yellow satin?"

"They're both so pretty, it's hard to choose. The yellow satin, I think; it's a dream of a frock."

Mrs. Perry wrote a most cordial invitation and also telephoned, saying how glad she would be to welcome Patty to her home.

And so, the next afternoon, the young people started on their motor trip.

It was easily accomplished in two hours, and then Patty found herself a very much honoured guest in Mrs. Perry's pleasant home.

"It's dear of you to come," said the vivacious little hostess, as she took Patty and Marie to their rooms upon their arrival.

"It's dear of you to ask me." returned Patty; "I love to go to parties, and I love to go into new people's hou- ses, - I mean people's new houses, - oh, well, you know what I mean; I mean HERE!"

"The house IS new," said Mrs. Perry, laughing, "but we're getting to be old people, and we want you young folks to liven us up."

"Old people!" and Patty smiled at the pretty young matron.

"Yes, wait till you see my baby. She's almost three years old! Fancy my going to balls, with a big girl like that."

"You're just fishing," said Patty, laughingly, "and I shan't humour you. I know you young mothers! You go to a party, and you're the belles, and leave all us wall-flowers green with envy!"

Mrs. Perry's eyes twinkled, and she looked so roguish that Patty exclaimed, "You're exactly like Mr. Cameron! I can well believe you're his sister."

"Who's he? Oh, you mean Kit! I don't think I ever heard him called Mr. Cameron before, and it does sound so funny! Can't we persuade you to say Kit?"

"I don't mind, if he doesn't," said Patty, carelessly. "What a darling room this is!"

"Yes; this is one of my pet rooms. I always give it to my favourite guests."

"I don't wonder," and Patty looked round admiringly at the dainty draperies and pretty appointments of the chamber.

"Marie always has it when she's here; but, of course, she was glad to give it up to you, and I put her in the blue room just across the hall. Come now, powder your nose, we must run down to tea. Don't change your frock."

Patty had worn a little silk house gown under her motor coat, so after a brief adjustment of her tumbled curls she was ready to go down.

The Perrys' was a modern house of an elaborate type. There were many rooms, on varying levels, so that one was continually going up or down a few broad steps. Often the rooms were separated only by columns or by railings, which made the whole interior diversified and picturesque.

"Such a gem of a house!" exclaimed Patty, as she entered the tea-room. "So many cosy, snuggly places, - and so warm and balmy."

She dropped into a lot of silken cushions that were piled in the corner of an inglenook, and placed her feet daintily on a footstool in front of the blazing fire.

"Awful dinky!" said Kit, as he pushed aside some cushions and sat down beside Patty, "but a jolly good house to visit in."

"Yes, it is," said Marie, who was nestled in an easy-chair the other side of the great fireplace. "And it's so light and pleasant. We never get any sunlight, home."

"Nonsense, Marie," said Kit, "our apartments are unusually light ones."

"Well, it's a different kind of light," protested Marie. "It only comes from across the street, and here the light comes clear from the horizon."

"It does," agreed Mrs. Perry, "but we're getting the very last rays now. Ring for lights, Kit."

"No, sister, let's just have the firelight. It's more becoming, anyway."

So Mrs. Perry merely turned on one pink-shaded light near the tea table and let her guests enjoy the twilight and firelight.

"Country life is 'way ahead of city existence," remarked Kenneth, as he made himself useful in passing the teacups. "The whole atmosphere is different. When I marry and settle down, I shall be a country gentleman."

"How interesting!" cried Patty. "I should love to see you, Ken, superintending your gardener and showing him how to plant cabbages!"

"Dead easy," retorted Kenneth; "I'd have a gardener show me first, and when the next gardener came I could show him."

"Well, I don't want to live in the country," said Kit;

"it's great to visit here, that's what sisters' houses are for; but I couldn't live so far away from the busy mart. Back to the stones for mine."

When their host, Dick Perry, arrived he came in with a genial, breezy manner and warmly welcomed the guests.

"Well, well!" he exclaimed, "this IS a treat! To come home at night and find a lot of gay and festive young people gathered around! Lora, why don't we do this oftener? Nothing like a lot of young people to make a home merry. How are you, Marie? Glad to see you again, Miss Fairfield."

Mr. Perry bustled around, flung off his coat, accepted a cup of tea from his wife, and then, coming over toward Patty, he ordered Kit Cameron to vacate, and he took his place.

"You're not to be monopolised by that brother-in-law of mine, Miss Fairfield," he said, as he sat down beside her. "He's a clever young chap, I admit, but he can't always get ahead of me."

Patty responded laughingly to this gay banter, and the tea hour passed all too quickly, and it was time to dress for dinner.

"We'll put on our party frocks before dinner," said Mrs. Perry, as she went upstairs with the girls; "and then we won't have to dress twice. I'll send you a maid, Miss Fairfield."

"Thank you," said Patty, "but I can look after myself fairly well, - until it comes to hooking up. I always do my own hair."

"It can't be much trouble," said Mrs. Perry, looking admiringly at the golden curls, "for it looks lovely whatever way you do it."

Patty slipped on a kimono and brushed out her shining mass of curls. As Mrs. Perry had rightly said, Patty's coiffure was not troublesome, for however she bunched up the gleaming mass it looked exactly right. She twisted it up with care, however, and added a marvellous ornament of a bandeau, which circled halfway round her head, and above which a gilt butterfly was tremblingly poised. It was too early to get into her frock, so Patty flung herself into a big chair before the crackling fire, and gave herself up to daydreams. She dearly loved to idle this way and she fell to thinking, naturally, of the home she was visiting and the people who lived there.

Patty still sat dreaming these idle fancies, when there was a tap at the door and, in response to her permission, a maid entered.

"I'm Babette," she said, "and I have come to help you with your gown."

"Thank you," said Patty, jumping up; "it's later than I thought. We must make haste."

With experienced deftness, the French maid arrayed Patty in the beautiful evening gown of yellow satin, veiled with a shimmering yellow gauze.

Although unusual for a blonde, yellow was exceedingly becoming to Patty, and she looked like an exquisite spring blossom in the soft, sheath-like jonquil-coloured gown.

Her dainty satin slippers and silk stockings were of the same pale yellow, as was also the filmy scarf, which she knew how to wear so gracefully.

Her only ornament was a string of pearls, which had been her mother's.

When she was all ready she went slowly down the winding staircase, looking about her at the interesting house. A broad landing halfway down showed an attractive window-seat, and Patty sat down there for a moment.

There seemed to be no one in the hall below, and Patty concluded that she was early after all, though she had feared she would be late.

In a moment Kit came down and spied her.

"Hello, Princess!" he cried. "You're a yellow poppy to-night, - and a gay little blossom, too."

"Not yellow poppyCHEEK!" cried Patty, rubbing her pink cheeks in mock dismay.

"Well, no; only one who is colour-blind could call those pink cheeks yellow. May I pose beside you, here, and make a beautiful tableau?"

He sat beside Patty on the window-seat, and they wondered why the rest were so late.

"Prinking, I suppose," said Kit. "How did you manage

to get ready so soon?"

"Why, just because I thought I was late, and so I hurried."

"Didn't know a girl COULD hurry, - accept my compliments." And Kit rose and made an exaggerated bow.

"What's going on?" said Dick Perry, gaily, as he came downstairs and paused on the landing.

"Only homage at the shrine of Beauty," returned Kit.

"Let me homage, too," said Mr. Perry, and they both bowed and scraped, until Patty went off in a gale of laughter and said: "You ridiculous boys, you look like popinjays! But here comes Marie; now more homage is due."

Marie came down the steps slowly and gracefully, looking very pretty in pale green, with tiny pink rosebuds for trimming.

"Good for you, Marie!" exclaimed her cousin. "Your dress gees with Miss Fairfield's first-rate. You'll do!"

And then the others came, and the merry group went out to dinner.

After dinner they started at once for the country-club ball. It was to be a very large affair, and, as Patty knew no one except their own house party, she declared that she knew she'd be a wall-flower.

"Wall-flower, indeed!" said Kit. "Poppies don't grow on walls. They grow right in the middle of the field, and sway and dance in the breeze."

"I always said you were a poet," returned Patty, "and you do have the prettiest fancies."

"I fancy YOU, if that's what you mean," Kit replied, and Patty gave him a haughty glance for his impertinence.

Then Babette put on Patty's coat, which was a really gorgeous affair. It was what is known as a Mandarin coat, of white silk, heavily embroidered with gold, and very quaint she looked in it.

"That thing must weigh a ton," commented Kit. "Why do you girls want to wear Chinese togs?"

"It's a beautiful coat," said Mrs. Perry, admiringly. "Have you been to China, Miss Fairfield?"

"No; I never have. This was a Christmas present, and I'm awfully fond of it. I'm afraid I'm barbaric in my love of bright, glittering things."

"A very civilised little barbarian," said Mr. Perry, and then they all went off to the ball.

"How many may I have?" said Kit, as he took Patty's programme from her hand after they were in the ballroom.

"As I don't know any one else, I shall have to dance them all with you and Ken," returned Patty, demurely.

"Never mind Harper; give them all to me."

Patty looked at him calmly. "I'll tell you what," she said: "you put down your initials for every dance; then, if I do find any partners I like better, I'll give them dances; and, if not, you see I'll have you to depend on."

Cameron stared at her, but Patty looked at him with an innocent smile, as if she were not asking anything extraordinary.

"Well, you've got a nerve!" the young man exclaimed.

"Why, it was your own proposition that you have all the dances;" and Patty looked almost offended.

"Poppycheek, you shall have it your own way! You shall have anything you want, that *I* can give you." And Cameron scribbled his initials against every one of the twenty dances on the programme.

"You might have put K. C. to the first and then ditto after that," said Patty, as she watched him.

"Nay, nay, Pauline!" and Kit gave her a shrewd glance. "Think what would happen then. You'd give a dance to some other man, maybe, and he'd set down his initials, and all the rest of the dittos would refer to him!"

"Poor man! I never thought of that! But it isn't likely there'll be any others except Ken."

"Oh, don't you worry! Everybody will want an introduction to you, after they see you dance."

"I don't think much of that for a compliment! I'd rather be loved for my sweet self alone."

"Have you never been?"

"Many, many times!" and Patty sighed in mock despair. "But my love affairs always end tragically."

"Your suitors drown themselves, I suppose?"

"Do you mean if I encourage them?"

"Do you know what a silly you are?"

"Do you know what a goose YOU are?"

"Children, stop quarrelling," and Mrs. Perry smiled at the chattering pair. "Miss Fairfield, several amiable young men of my acquaintance desire to be presented to you. May I?"

Patty smilingly acquiesced, and in a moment half a dozen would-be partners were asking for dances.

They looked rather taken aback at sight of Patty's card, but she calmly explained to them the true condition of things, and they accepted the situation with smiles of admiration for a girl who could command such an arrangement. Patty would not give more than one dance to each, as she wanted to find out which ones she liked best.

Mr. Perry brought up some of his acquaintances, too, and shortly Patty's programme showed an astonishing lot of hieroglyphics scribbled over Kit's initials.

"Here are twelve dances you may have for your other friends," said Patty, to Mr. Cameron. "Take the numbers as I call them off: one, two, three -"

"Oh, wait a minute! Have you given them all away?"

"No; only the first twelve, so far. But cheer up! I may be able to dispose of the others."

"You're a naughty, bad, mean little princess; and I don't love you any more."

Kit looked reproachfully at Patty, with his eyes so full of disappointment that she relented.

"I didn't give away the first one, really," she said, softly. "I saved that for you."

"You blessed, dear, sweet little Princess you! Now, don't give away any more, will you? I know you'll have thousands of requests."

"I'll see about it," was all Patty would promise, and then the music began and they stepped out on to the dancing floor.

CHAPTER IX

EDDIE BELL

Which do you like best of all the boys you've met?" asked Kit, as they danced.

"What a question! How can I possibly tell, when a dozen well-behaved and serious-looking young men stand up like a class in school and say, one after another, 'May I have the honour of a dance, Miss Fairfield?' They all looked exactly alike to me. Except one. There was one boy, who looks so much like me he might be my brother. I never had a brother, and I've a good notion to adopt him as one."

"Don't! There's nothing so dangerous as adopting a young man for a brother! But I know who you mean, - Eddie Bell. He doesn't look a bit like you, but he HAS yellow curls and blue eyes."

"And pink cheeks," supplemented Patty.

"Yes, but not poppy cheeks; they're more the pink of a - of a - horsechestnut!"

"I think pink horsechestnut blooms are beautiful."

"Oh, you do, do you? And I suppose you think Eddie

Carolyn Wells

Bell is beautiful!"

"Well, there's no occasion for you to get mad about it if I do. Do you know, Mr. Cameron, you flare up very easily."

"If you'll call me Kit, I'll promise never to flare up again."

"Certainly, I'll call you Kit. I'd just as lieve as not; anything to oblige."

"And may I call you Patty?"

"Why, yes, if you like."

"Look here, you're altogether too indifferent about it."

"Oh, what a boy!" And Patty rolled her eyes up in despair. "If I don't want him to call me Patty, he doesn't like it; and if I do let him call me Patty, he isn't satisfied! What to do, - what to do!"

"You're a little tease, - THAT'S what you are!"

"And you're a big tease, that's what YOU are! I've heard you're even fond of practical jokes! Now, I detest practical jokes."

"That's an awful pity, for I mean to play one on you the very first chance I get."

"You can't do it?"

"Why can't I?"

"Because I'd discover it, and foil you."

"There's no such word as foil in my bright lexicon. I'll lay you a wager, if you like, that I play a practical joke on you, that you, yourself, will admit is clever and not unkind. That's the test of a right kind of a joke, - to be clever and not unkind."

Patty's eyes danced. "You have the right idea about it," she said, nodding her head approvingly. "I don't so much mind a practical joke, if it is really a good one, and doesn't make the victim feel hurt or chagrined. But all the same, Mr. Kit, you can't get one off on me! I'm a little too wide-awake, as you'll find out."

"Would you take a wager?"

"I'm not in the habit of betting, but I'm willing for once. It's hardly fair, though, for I'm betting on a dead certainty."

"You mean you THINK you are! And I think *I* am, so the chances are even. What are the stakes?"

"I don't care: candy or books or flowers or anything."

"Nonsense, they're too prosaic. If I win, you're to give me a photograph of yourself."

"Oh, I almost never give my picture to my suitors. It isn't good form."

"But, if you're so sure that you will win, you needn't be afraid to promise it."

"All right, I promise; and, if I win, you may give me a

perfectly beautiful picture frame, in which I shall put some other man's picture."

"How cruel you can be! But, as I'm sure of winning, I'm not afraid to take that up. A frame against a picture, then. But there must be a time limit."

"I'll give you a month; if you can't do it in that time, you can't do it at all. And, also, I must be the judge, - if you do fool me, - whether your practical joke is clever and not unkind."

"I'm quite contented that you should be the judge, for I know your sincere and honest nature will not let you swerve a hair's breadth from a true and fair judgment."

"That's clever," returned Patty; "for now I shall have to be honest."

The first dance over, Patty went on with a long succession of dances with her various partners. They were all polite and courteous young men, some attractive and agreeable, others shy, and some dull and uninteresting. Patty complacently accorded another dance to any one she liked, and calmly refused it to less desirable partners, - pleading an engagement with Cameron as her excuse.

The one she liked best was Eddie Bell. As she had said, this young man did look a little like Patty herself, though this was mostly due to their similarity of colouring.

"If I may say anything so impossible, it seems to me that I look like a comic valentine of you," said Mr. Bell, as they began to dance.

Patty laughed outright at this apt expression of their resemblance, and said: "I have already told some one that you looked exactly like me. So, in that case, I'm a comic valentine, too. But, truly, you're enough like me to be my brother."

"May I be? Not that I want to, in the least, but of course that is the obvious thing to say. I'd rather be most any relation to you than a brother."

"Why?"

"Oh, it's such a prosaic relationship. I have three sisters, - and they're the dearest girls in the world, - but I don't really feel the need of any more."

"What would you like to be?" And Patty flashed him a dangerous glance of her pansy-blue eyes.

But Mr. Bell kept his equanimity. "How about second cousin, once removed?"

"I suppose you'll be removed at the end of this dance."

"Then, may this dance last for ever!"

"Oh, what a pretty speech! Of course, you wouldn't make that to a sister! I think a second cousinship is very pleasant."

"Then, that's settled. And I may call you Cousin Patty, I suppose?"

"It would seem absurd to say Cousin Miss Fairfield, wouldn't it? And yet our acquaintance is entirely too short for first names."

"But it's growing longer every minute; and, if you would grant me another dance after I'm removed from this one, I'm sure we could reach the stage of first names."

"I will give you one more," said Patty, for she liked Mr. Bell very much.

So at the end of their dance they agreed upon a number later on the programme, and Mr. Bell wrote down "Cousin Ed" on Patty's card.

It was just after this that Kit came back for his second dance.

"Naughty girl," he said; "you've kept me waiting three-quarters of the evening."

"I thought I saw you dancing with several visions of beauty."

"Only killing time till I could get back to you. Come on, don't waste a minute."

It was a joy to Patty to dance with Cameron, for he was by all odds the best dancer she had ever met. And many admiring glances followed them as they circled the great room.

"How did you like your little brother?" Kit enquired.

"He's a ducky-daddles!" declared Patty, enthusiastically. "Just a nice all-round boy, frank and jolly and good-natured."

"That's what I am."

"Not a bit of it! You're a musician; freakish, temperamental, touchy, and - a woman-hater."

"Gracious! what a character to live up to, - or down to. But I hate YOU awfully, don't I?"

"I don't know. I never can feel sure of these temperamental natures."

"Well, don't you worry about feeling sure of me. The longer you live, the surer you'll feel."

"That sounds like 'the longer she lives the shorter she grows,'" said Patty, flippantly.

"Yes, the old nursery rhyme. Well, you are my candle, - a beacon, lighting my pathway with your golden beams -"

"Oh, do stop! That's beautiful talk, but it's such rubbish."

"Haven't you ever noticed that much beautiful talk IS rubbish?"

"Yes, I have. And I'm glad that you think that way, too. Beautiful thoughts are best expressed by plain, sincere words, and have little connection with 'beautiful talk.'"

"Patty Fairfield, you're a brick! And, when I've said that, I can't say anything more."

"A gold brick?"

"Not in the usual acceptance of that term; but you're pure gold, and I'm jolly well glad I've found a girl like you."

There was such a ring of sincerity in Cameron's tone that Patty looked up at him suddenly. And the honest look in his eyes made it impossible for her to return any flippant response.

"And I'm glad, too, that we are friends, Kit," she said, simply.

The next dance was Mr. Bell's, and that rosy-cheeked youth came up blithely to claim it.

"Come along, Cousin Patty," he said, and Cameron stared at him in amazement.

"Are you two cousins?" he said.

"Once removed," returned Eddie Bell, gaily; "and this is the removal." He took Patty's hand and laid it lightly within his own arm as he led her away.

"Don't let's dance right off," he begged. "Let's rest a minute in this bosky dell."

The dell was an alcove off the ballroom, which contained several palms and floral baskets and a deep, cushioned window-seat.

"Let's sit here and watch the moon rise;" and he led Patty toward the window-seat, where he deftly arranged some cushions for her.

"I believe the moon rises to-morrow afternoon," said Patty.

"Well, I don't mind waiting. Sit here, won't you? These stupid cushions ought to be of a golden yellow or a pale green. However, this old rose does fairly well for our blond beauty. Isn't it nice we're of the same type and harmonise with the same furnishings? When we're married we won't have to differ about our house decorations." "When we are WHAT?"

"Married, I said. You know, you're not really my second cousin and there's absolutely no bar to our union."

This was quite the most audacious young man Patty had ever met. But she was quite equal to the situation.

"Of course there isn't," she said, lightly. "And, when I think of the economy of our being able to use the same colour scheme, it IS an inducement."

"And meantime we must get better acquainted, as you said when we were dancing. May I come to see you in the city? Where do you live?"

"In Seventy-second Street," said Patty, "but I feel it my duty to tell you that there's already a long line awaiting admission."

"Oh, yes, I've seen that line when I've been passing. It goes clear round the corner of the block. Do I have to take my place at the end, or can I have a special favour shown me?"

"I'm sure your sense of justice wouldn't permit that. You take your place at the end of the line, and when your turn comes I'll be glad to welcome you."

"Then that's all right," said Mr. Bell, cheerfully, "and you'll be surprised to see how soon I appear! Now, lady fair, would you rather go and dance or sit here and listen to me converse?"

"It's pleasant to rest a little," and Patty nestled into her cushions, "and you really ARE amusing, you know. Let's stay here a little while."

"Now, isn't that nice of you! Do you want to talk, too, or shall I do it all and give you a complete rest?"

"You do it all," said Patty, indolently. "It will be like going to a monologue entertainment."

"At your orders. What subject would you like?"

"Yourself."

"Oh, wise beyond your years! You know the subject that most interests a man."

"That isn't pretty!" And Patty frowned at him. "There ought to be another subject more interesting to you than that!"

"There is; but I don't dare trust myself with HER!"

Mr. Bell's manner and voice were so exactly the right mixture of deferential homage and burlesque that Patty laughed in delight.

"You are the DEAREST man!" she cried.

He looked at her reproachfully. "You said I might do all the talking, and now you're doing it yourself."

"I'll be still now. Avoid that subject you consider dangerous and tell me all about yourself."

"Well, once upon a time, there was a beautiful young man who rejoiced in the poetic and musical name of Eddie Bell. I know he was a beautiful young man, because he was said to resemble the most beautiful girl in the whole world. Well, one evening he had the supreme good fortune to meet this girl, and he realised at once that he had met his Fate, - his Fate with a VERY large F. Incidentally, the F stood for Fairfield, which made his Fate all the more certain. And so -"

"Patty, are you here?" and Ken Harper came through the palms toward them. "This is our dance."

"Good gracious, Ken, is this dance the next dance? I mean is this dance over, or is this dance our dance."

"You seem a little mixed, Patty, but this is our dance and I claim it. Are you RESTED enough?"

Patty rose and, with a simple word of excuse to Mr. Bell, went away with Kenneth.

"That's the first time, Ken, in all our friendship that I ever knew you to say anything horrid," and Patty looked at him with a really hurt expression.

"I didn't say anything horrid," and Kenneth's fine face wore a sulky expression.

"You did, too. You asked me if I were RESTED in a horrid, sarcastic tone; and you meant it for a reproof, because I sat out that dance with Mr. Bell."

"You had no business to go and hide behind those palms with him."

"We didn't hide! That's only a bay-window alcove, - a part of the ballroom. I have a perfect right to sit out a dance if I choose."

"That young chap was too familiar, anyway. I heard him calling you 'Cousin Patty.'"

"Oh, fiddlestrings, Ken! Don't be an idiot! We were only joking. And I'm not so old, yet, but what I can let a boy call me by my first name if I choose. When I'm twenty I'm going to be Miss Fairfield; but while I'm nineteen anybody can call me Patty, - if I give him permission."

"You're a flirt, Patty."

"All right, Ken. Flirt with me, won't you?" Patty's roguish blue eyes looked at Kenneth with such a frank and friendly glance that he couldn't scold her any more.

"I can't flirt with you, Patty. I'm not that sort. You know very well I've only a plain, plodding sort of a mind, and I can't keep up with this repartee and persiflage that you carry on with these other chaps."

"I don't carry on," said Patty, laughing.

"I didn't say you carried on," returned Kenneth, who took everything seriously. "I meant you carried on conversations that are full of wit and repartee, of a sort that I can't get off."

"Nobody wants you to, you dear old Ken! You wouldn't be half as nice if you were as foolish and frivolous as these society chatterboxes! You've got more sterling worth and real intellect in your make-up than they ever dreamed of. Now, stop your nonsense and come on and dance. But - don't undertake to lecture Patty Fairfield, - she won't stand for it!"

"I didn't mean to lecture you, Patty," and Kenneth spoke very humbly. "But when I saw you tucked away behind those palms, flirting with that yellow-headed rattle-pate, I felt that I ought to speak to you."

"You SPOKE, all right!" and Patty looked at him severely. "But you know perfectly well, Kenneth Harper, that I wasn't doing anything I oughtn't to. You know perfectly well that, though I like what you call 'flirting,' I'm never the least bit unconventional and I never forget the strictest law of etiquette and propriety. I'd scorn to do such a thing!"

Patty's blue eyes were blazing now with righteous indignation, for Kenneth had been unjust, and Patty would not stand injustice. She was punctilious in matters of etiquette, and she had not overstepped any bounds by sitting out a dance in that alcove, which was a part of the ballroom and a refuge for any one weary of dancing.

"And you know perfectly well, Kenneth," she went on, "that you DIDN'T think I was unconventional, or anything of the sort. You were only -"

Patty paused, for she didn't quite want to say what was in her mind.

"You're right, Little Patty," and Kenneth looked her straight in the eyes; "you're right. I WAS jealous. Yes, and envious. It always hurts me to see you laughing and talking in that darling little way of yours, and to know that *I* can't make you talk like that. I wish I weren't such a stupid-head! I wish *I* could say things that would make you play your pretty fooleries with ME."

Patty looked at him in amazement. She had never suspected that serious-minded, hard-working Kenneth had anything but scorn for men of less mental calibre and quicker wit.

"Why, Kenneth," she said, gently, "don't talk like that. My friendship for you is worth a dozen of these silly foolery flirtations with men that I don't care two cents for."

"I don't want your friendship, Patty," and Kenneth's deep voice trembled a little; "I mean I don't want ONLY your friendship. And yet I know I can't hope for anything more. I'm too dull and commonplace to attract a beautiful butterfly like you."

"Kenneth," and Patty gave him a glance, gentle, but a little bewildered, "you're out of your head. You have a splendid head, Kenneth, full of wonderful brains, but you're out of it. You get yourself back into it as quick as you can! And don't let's dance this dance, please; I am tired. I wish you'd take me to Mrs. Perry."

In silence, Kenneth complied with Patty's wish, and took her to where Lora Perry was sitting.

Then he went away, leaving Patty much more

disturbed by what he had said than by all the gay fooleries of Eddie Bell or Kit Cameron.

CHAPTER X

QUARANTINED

"Tired?" asked Mrs. Perry, as she welcomed Patty to her side.

"A little; I love to dance, but a long program does weary me. Are we going home soon?"

"Whenever you like, dear."

"Oh, not until the others are ready. There goes Marie. She's having a lovely time to-night. Isn't she a pretty thing? - and so popular."

Patty's admiration was sincere and honest, and Marie's dark, glowing beauty was well worthy of commendation.

But seeing Patty sitting by Mrs. Perry, Marie came to them, when the dance ended, and declared that she was quite ready to go home, although the program wasn't finished.

"What's all this about?" inquired Kit Cameron, coming up to them. "Go home? Not a bit of it! There are a lot of dances yet."

"Well, you stay for them if you like, Kit," said his sister, rising. "I'm going to take these girls away. They've danced quite enough, and it's time they went home."

"Whither thou all goest, I will go also," said Cameron. "Where's Harper?"

Kenneth and Dick Perry came along then, and both men expressed their willingness to go home.

Patty was rather silent during the homeward way, and indeed, as all were more or less weary, there was little gay conversation.

As they entered the house, Nora, the parlour-maid, appeared to take their wraps.

"Where is Babette?" asked Mrs. Perry, surprised to see Nora in place of her French maid.

"Sure she's sick, Mrs. Perry; she do be feelin' that bad, she had to go to bed. So she bid me do the best I can for the young ladies."

"I'm sorry to hear Babette is ill; I must go and see her at once." And Mrs. Perry went away toward the servants' quarters.

She returned shortly, saying Babette had a bad cold and a slight fever, but that her symptoms were not alarming.

"But I'm sorry you girls can't have her services to-night," Mrs. Perry went on.

"It doesn't matter a bit," said Patty; "I'd be sorry for myself, if I couldn't get in and out of my own clothes! Don't think of it, Mrs. Perry."

They all went up to their rooms, and though Nora did her best to assist Patty, her unskilful help bothered more than it aided. So she kindly dismissed the girl, and catching up a kimono went across to Marie's room.

"You get me out of this frock, won't you, Marie?" she said. "It fidgets me to have Nora fumbling with the hooks. It's a complicated arrangement and I know she'd tear the lace."

Marie willingly acquiesced, and then Patty slipped off the pretty yellow gown, and got into her blue silk kimono.

"Stay here and brush out your hair, Patty," said Marie, "and we can have a 'kimono chat,' all by ourselves."

So Patty sat down at Marie's toilet table, and began to brush out her golden curls.

"Did you like the ball, Patty?" asked Marie, as she braided her own dark hair.

"Lovely! Everybody was so nice to me. And you had a good time yourself, I know. I saw you breaking hearts, one after another, you little siren."

"Siren, yourself! How did you like that Bell boy?"

"Gracious! That sounds like a hotel attendant! In fact I think 'bellhop,' as I believe they call them, wouldn't be a bad name for Eddie Bell. I liked him ever so much, but he was a little, - well, - fresh is the only word that expresses it."

"He is cheeky; but he doesn't mean anything. He's a nice boy; I've known him for years. He's an awful flirt, - but he admired you like everything. Though as to that, who doesn't?"

"Oh, I don't think so much of this general admiration. I think if a young girl isn't admired, it's her own fault. She only has to be gay and pleasant and good-natured, and people are bound to like her."

"Yes," agreed Marie; "but there are degrees. I'll tell you who likes you an awful lot, - and that's Mr. Harper."

"Oh, Kenneth;" Patty spoke carelessly, but she couldn't prevent a rising blush. "Why, Marie, we've been chums for years. I used to know Ken Harper when I was a little girl and lived in Vernondale. He's a dear boy, but we're just good friends."

"I like him," and Marie said this so ingenuously, that Patty gave her a quick look. "Don't you like anybody ESPECIALLY, Patty?"

"No, I don't. All boys look alike to me. I like to have them to dance with, and to send me flowers and candy; and I don't mind make-believe flirting with them; but the minute they get serious, I want to run away."

"Aren't you ever going to be engaged, Patty?"

"Nonsense! Marie, we're too young to think about such things. After a few years I shall begin to consider the matter; and if I find anybody that I simply can't live without, I shall proceed to marry him. Now, curiosity-box, is there anything else you want to know?"

"I didn't mean to be curious," and Marie's pretty face looked troubled; "but, Patty, I will ask you one more question: Couldn't you, - couldn't you like, - specially, I mean, - my cousin Kit?"

"Marie, I've a notion to shake you! You little match-maker, - or mischief-maker, - stop getting notions into your head! In the first place, I've known your paragon of a cousin only a few weeks; and in the second place, there's no use going any further than the first place! Now, you go to sleep, and dream about birds and flowers and sunshine, and don't fill your pretty head with grown-up notions."

"You're a funny girl, Patty," and Marie looked at her with big, serious eyes.

"If it's funny to be a common-sense, rational human being, then I AM funny! Now, good-night, chicka-biddy. Mrs. Perry says she'll send up our breakfast about nine to-morrow morning. Hop into my room and have it with me, won't you?"

Marie agreed to this arrangement, and gathering up her belongings, Patty slipped across the hall to her own room.

The wood fire had burnt down to red embers, and lowering the lights, Patty sat down for a few moments in a big fireside chair to think.

She had told the truth, that she did not want to think

seriously of what Marie called "an especial liking" for anybody; but what Kenneth had said that evening troubled her.

Her friendship for Kenneth was so firm and strong, her real regard for him so deep and sincere, that she hated to have it intruded upon by a question of a more serious feeling. And she had never suspected that any such question would arise. But she could not mistake the meaning of Kenneth's spoken wish that he might be capable of the gay conversation in which Patty delighted.

"Dear old Ken," she said to herself, "he's so nice just as he is, but when he tries to be funny, he - well, he CAN'T, that's all. It isn't his fault. All the boys can't be alike. And I s'pose Ken IS the nicest of them, after all. He's so true and reliable. But I hope to gracious he isn't going to fall in love with me. That would spoil everything I Oh, well, I won't cross that bridge until I come to it. And if I have come to it, - well, I won't cross it, even then. I'll just stand stock-still, and wait. I believe there's a poem somewhere, that says:

> "'Standing with reluctant feet
> Where the brook and river meet, -
> Womanhood and childhood sweet.'

"I s'pose I HAVE left childhood behind, but I feel a long way off from womanhood. And yet, in a couple of months I'll be twenty. That does begin to sound aged! But I know one thing, sure and certain: I'll wait till I AM twenty, before I think about a serious love affair. Suitors are all very well, but I wouldn't be engaged to a man for anything! Why, I don't suppose he'd let me dance with anybody else, or have any fun at all! No,

Carolyn Wells

sir-ee, Patricia Fairfield, you're going to have two or three years of your present satisfactory existence, before you wear anybody's diamond ring. And now, my Lady Gay, you'd better skip to bed, for to-morrow night you have a theatre party in prospect, and you want to look fairly decent for that."

The fire was burnt out now, and Patty was so sleepy that her head had scarcely touched the pillow before she fell asleep.

A light tap at her door awakened her the next morning, and Marie appeared, followed by Nora, with a breakfast tray.

"Wake up, curly-head-sleepy-head," and Marie play-fully tweaked Patty's curls. "Here, I'll be your maid. Here's your nightingale, and here's your breakfast cap."

Marie deftly arrayed Patty in the pretty trifles, and poked pillows behind her back until she was comfortable.

"Goodness gracious sakes! Marie," said Patty, rubbing her eyes, "you waked me out of the soundest sleep I have ever known! WHY bother me with breakfast?"

"Had to do it," returned Marie, calmly, drawing up a big chair for herself. "Now keep your eyes open and behave like a lady. Your chocolate is getting cool and your toast is spoiling."

The two girls were still discussing their breakfast, when Mrs. Perry came in.

" How are you getting on ? " she asked , cheerily;

"Babette is still ill, so I had to send Nora to you."

"Everything is lovely," said Patty, smiling at her hostess. "We're delightfully looked after. Nora is a jewel. But I hope your maid isn't seriously ill."

"I'm afraid she is," and Mrs. Perry looked troubled. "She has a bad sore throat and she's quite feverish. Now you girlies dawdle around as much as you like. Although I'm commissioned to tell you that there are two young men downstairs just pining for you, and they asked me to coax you to come down at once."

"Let them wait," said Patty; "we'll be down after a while. Mayn't we see the baby?"

"Yes, indeed, if you like. I'll send her in."

Soon a dainty little morsel of fragrant humanity appeared, accompanied by her nurse.

The tot was a trifle shy, but Patty's merry smile soon put her at her ease.

"Tell the lady your name, dear," said Marie.

"Pitty Yady!" said the baby, caressing Patty's cheek.

"Yes," said Marie, "now tell the pretty lady your name."

"Baby Boo," said the child.

"Baby Boo! What a dear name!" said Patty.

" Her name is Beulah , " Marie explained, "but she

always calls herself Baby Boo, so every one else does."

"It's just the name for her," said Patty, catching up the midget in her arms and cuddling her.

"Pitty Yady," repeated the baby, gazing at Patty.

"She's struck with your beauty, Patty, like everybody else," said Marie, laughing.

"It's mutual, then," returned Patty, "for I think she's the prettiest baby I ever saw. And she does smell so good! I love a violet baby." And Patty kissed the back of the soft little neck and squeezed the baby up in her arms.

"Now Baby Boo must go away," said Marie, at last, "for the Pitty Yady must get dressed and go downstairs."

Patty had brought a morning frock, of pink linen with a black velvet sash, and she looked very trim and sweet as she at last declared herself ready.

The two girls went downstairs, and found two very impatient young men awaiting them.

"Whatever HAVE you girls been doing all the morning?" exclaimed Cameron; "you CAN'T have been sleeping until this time!"

"Playing with the baby, and exchanging confidences," said Patty, smiling.

"Both of which you might as well have done down here," Cameron declared. "I adore my baby niece, and

Mr. Harper and I would have been more than glad to listen to your exchange of confidences."

"Oh, they weren't intended for your ears!" exclaimed Marie, with mock horror. "Kimono confidences are very, VERY sacred. But it may well be that your ears burn."

"Which ear?" asked Kenneth, feeling of both of his.

"Fair exchange," said Marie, gaily. "Tell us what you said about us, and we'll tell you what we said about you."

"We said you were the two prettiest and sweetest girls in the world," said Cameron.

"And we said," declared Patty, "that you were the two handsomest and most delightful men in the world."

"But we said you had some faults," said Kenneth, gravely.

"And we said you had," retorted Marie. "Let's tell each other our faults. That's always an interesting performance, for it always winds up with a quarrel."

"I love a quarrel," said Cameron, enthusiastically. "I dare anybody to tell me my greatest faults!"

"Conceit," said Marie, smiling at her cousin.

"That isn't a fault; it's a virtue," Kit retorted.

"That's so," and Marie nodded her head; "if you didn't have that virtue, you wouldn't have any."

"That's a facer!" said Kit. "Well, Marie, my dear, as you haven't THAT virtue, am I to conclude you haven't any?"

"That's very pretty," and Patty nodded, approvingly; "but I want to stop this game before it's my turn, for I'm too sensitive to have my faults held up to the public eye."

"But we haven't quarrelled yet," said Kit, who looked disappointed. "Why do you like to quarrel so much?" asked Patty.

"Because it's such fun to kiss and make up."

"Is it?" asked Patty; "I'd like to see it done, then. You and Ken quarrel, and then let us see you kiss and make up."

"Harper is too good-natured to quarrel and I'm not good-natured enough to kiss him," said Kit. "I guess I won't quarrel to-day, after all. I can't seem to get the right partner. Let's try some other game. Want to go over to the club and bowl?"

"Yes, indeed," cried Patty; "I'd love to."

So the four young people bundled into fur coats, and motored over to the country club.

They were all good players and enjoyed their game till Kit reminded them that it was nearly luncheon time, and they went back to the house.

"How is Babette?" Patty inquired, as their hostess appeared at luncheon.

"She's worse;" and Mrs. Perry looked very anxious. "I don't want to worry you girls, but I think you would better go home this afternoon, for I don't know what Babette's case may develop into. The doctor was here this morning, and he has sent a trained nurse to take care of the girl. I confess I am worried."

"Oh, we were going this afternoon, anyway," said Patty. "I have to, as I have an engagement this evening. But I'm sorry for you, Mrs. Perry. It is awful to have illness in the house. What is it you are afraid of?"

"I hate to mention it, but the doctor fears diphtheria. Now don't be alarmed, for there is positively no danger, if you go this afternoon. But I can't risk your staying an hour longer than is necessary. Nora will help you pack your things. And I'm going to send you off right after lunch."

After luncheon the doctor came again, and Mrs. Perry went off to confer with him.

"Excuse me," said Kit Cameron, as his sister left the room, "I must stand by Lora, and I want to find out from the doctor if there is really any danger. Perhaps my sister's fears are exaggerated."

It was nearly half an hour before Kit came back, and then he looked extremely serious.

"I have bad news for you," he said; "Babette's illness is diphtheria, - a severe case."

"Oh, the poor girl!" said Patty, with impulsive sympathy.

"Yes, indeed, little Babette is pretty sick. And, too, it's awfully hard on Lora. But that isn't all of it."

"What else?" said Marie, breathless with suspense.

"I hardly know how to tell you," and Cameron's face was very troubled. "But I suppose the best way is to tell you straight out. The truth is, we are all quarantined. We can't go away from here."

"Quarantined!" cried Patty, who knew that this meant several weeks' imprisonment; "oh, NO!"

"Yes," and Kit looked at her with pained eyes; "can you ever forgive me, Miss Fairfield, for bringing you here? But of course I could not foresee this awful climax to our pleasant party."

"Of course you couldn't!" cried Patty; - "don't think for a moment that we blame you, Mr. Cameron. But, - you must excuse me if I feel rather - rather -"

"Flabbergasted," put in Kenneth; "it's an awful thing, Cameron, but we must take it philosophically. Brace up, Patty girl, don't let this thing floor you."

Patty gave one look into Kenneth's eyes, and read there so much sympathy, courage, and strong helpfulness, that she was ashamed of herself.

"Forgive me for being so selfish," she said, as the tears came into her eyes. "Of course we must stay, if the doctor orders; I know how strict they have to be about these things. And we will stay cheerfully, as long as we must. It's dreadful to impose on Mrs. Perry so, but we can't help it, and we must simply make the best of it. We'll help her all we can, and I'm sure Marie and I can do a lot."

"You're a brick!" and Cameron gave her a look of appreciation. "Poor Lora is heart-broken at the trouble it makes for you girls, and for Harper. She quite loses sight of her own anxieties in worrying about you all."

"Tell her to stop it," said Marie; "I rather think that we can bear our part of it, considering what Cousin Lora has to suffer. Can Cousin Dick come home?"

"I hadn't thought of that!" exclaimed Cameron. "Why, no; that is, if he can't go back to his office again. We'll have to telephone him to stay in New York until the siege is raised. There are many things to think of, but as I am responsible for bringing you people up here, naturally that worries me the most. I'm not to blame for the maid's illness or for Dick's enforced absence from home. But I AM to blame for bringing you girls up here at all."

"Don't talk of blame, Mr. Cameron, please," said Patty's soft voice; "you kindly brought us here to give us pleasure and you did so. The fact that this emergency has arisen is of no blame to anybody. The only one to be blamed is the one who cannot meet it bravely!"

CHAPTER XI

MEETING IT BRAVELY

"You're the most wonderful girl in the world!" exclaimed Cameron, in a burst of admiration at Patty's speech.

But Kenneth looked steadily at Patty, with a thoughtful gaze.

"You're keyed up," he said to her, gently; "and if you take it like that, you'll collapse."

"Like what?" Patty snapped out the words, for her nerves were strung to a high tension.

"Doing the hysterical histrionic act," and Kenneth smiled at the excited girl, not reprovingly, but with gentle sympathy. "Now take it standing, Patty, - face it squarely, - and you'll be all right. We're housed up here, - for how long, Cameron?"

"I - I don't know," said Kit, looking desperate.

"That only means you won't tell," declared his cousin. "Own up, Kit, how long did the doctor say?"

"Three or four weeks."

"Oh!" Patty merely breathed the word, but it sounded like a wail of despair. Then she caught Kenneth's eye, and his glance of steadfast courage nerved her anew.

"It's all right," she said, almost succeeding in keeping a quiver out of her voice. "We can have a real good time. People can send us all sorts of things, and, - I suppose we can't write letters, - but we can telephone. Oh, that reminds me; may I telephone Mr. Van Reypen at once, that I can't" - Patty blinked her eyes, and swallowed hard - "that I can't be at my - at his party this evening?"

Mr. Cameron looked a picture of abject grief.

"Miss Fairfield," he began, "if I could only tell you how sorry I am -"

"Please don't," said Patty, kindly; "I've accepted the situation now, and you won't hear a single wail of woe from me. Pooh! what's a theatre party more or less among me! And a few weeks' rest will do us all good. We'll pretend we're at a rest cure or sanitarium, and go to bed early, and get up late, and all that."

"Oh, of course we must all telephone to our homes," said Marie; "and I must say, I think girls are selfish creatures! We've never given a thought to Mr. Harper's business!"

"Don't give it a thought," said Kenneth, lightly. "I've given it one or two already, and I may give it another. That's enough for any old business."

"That sounds well, Ken," said Patty, "but I know it's going to make you a terrific lot of trouble. And Mr. Cameron, too! A civil engineer -"

"Can't be uncivil, even in a case like this," put in Kit; "or I'd say what I really feel about the whole business! It would be worse, of course, if one of our own people were ill; but to be tied up like this because of a servant is, to say the least, exasperating."

"Babette's a nice little thing, and I'm awfully sorry for her," said Patty.

"So am I," said Marie; "but I'm like Kit. I think it's awful for half a dozen of us to be held here, like this, because a maid is ill!"

"But, Marie, what's the use of even thinking about it?" said Patty; "we can't help ourselves, we're obliged to stay here, so for goodness' sake, let's make the best of it. I shall send home for my pink chiffon, - that's always a great comfort to me in time of trouble."

"Send for one for me," said Cameron, "if they're so comforting in trouble."

"I've only one," returned Patty, "but you can share the benefit of its comforting qualities. Now we'll have to take turns at the telephone. Suppose I take it first, and break the news to Mr. Van Reypen, for he'll have to invite somebody in my place."

"You're sure it's positive?" said Kenneth to Cameron; "you're sure there's no hope of a reprieve or a mistaken diagnosis?"

"No," said Kit, positively; "I made sure, before I told you at all."

"Of course you did," said Patty, trying to be cheerful.

"I know you wouldn't have told us, until you were sure you had to. Now I'll telephone to Phil, and then to my home, and then, Marie, you can tell your people, and after that we'll let the men fix up their business affairs. What a comfort it is that we can telephone, for I don't suppose we'll be allowed to write letters, unless we fumigate them, and I won't inflict my friends with those horrid odours."

The telephone was in the library, and as Patty crossed the hall, she met Mrs. Perry coming toward her.

Mrs. Perry had her handkerchief to her eyes, and Patty went straight to her and put her arms around her.

"Dear Mrs. Perry," she said, "I am SO sorry for you! To have Babette's illness, and then to have the burden of four guests at the same time! But, truly, we'll make just as little trouble as we can, and I hope you'll let us help in any way possible."

"Oh, Patty," Lora Perry said, in a choked voice, "I feel dreadful about making you stay here in these circumstances! Just think of all your engagements, - and all the fun you'll miss. It's perfectly awful!"

"Now don't think of those things at all. Just remember that your four guests are not complaining a bit. We know you're sorry for us and you know we're sorry for you, and we're all sorry for poor Babette. Now that part's settled, and we're all going to make the best of it. You don't go into Babette's room, do you?"

"Oh, no; I couldn't go near the baby, if I did. And the patient has a trained nurse, you know. Honestly, Patty, - you don't mind my calling you Patty, do you?"

"No, indeed, I like to have you."

"Well, I was going to say, I don't really think there's a bit of danger of infection for any of us. But, of course, you know what a doctor's orders are, and how they must be obeyed."

"Of course I know; now don't you think for a moment of any petty little disappointments we girls may have. Why, they're nothing compared to your trouble and Mr. Perry's, and the boys'."

Patty telephoned Philip Van Reypen, and that young man was simply aghast.

"I can't believe it!" he exclaimed. "Do you mean to say that you people are to be held up there for weeks? It's preposterous! It's criminal!"

"Don't talk like that, Philip. We can't help it. The Perrys can't help it. And it isn't a national catastrophe. Honestly, a few weeks' rest will do me good."

"Yes! With that Cameron man dangling at your heels!"

"Well, Philip, if I have to stay here, you ought to be glad I have some one here to amuse me."

"I'm not! I'd rather you were there alone! Patty, I won't stand it! I'm coming up myself, to dig you out!"

"Don't talk foolishness! If you come up here, you'll have to stay! They don't let any one leave the house."

"All right, then, I'll stay! That wouldn't be half bad."

"Philip, behave yourself! Mrs. Perry has all the company she can take care of."

"I'll help her take care of her company. One of 'em, anyway!"

"I won't talk to you, if you're so silly. Now listen. You go ahead with your party to-night, and ask some other pretty girl to take my place."

"Take your place!" Philip's growl of disgust nearly broke the telephone.

"Yes," went on Patty, severely, "to take my place. And then, when we get let out, you could have another party for me. Don't you see, it will be a sort of celebration of my release from captivity."

"I tell you I won't stand it! I'll have the confounded party to-night, - because I'll HAVE to, but to-morrow I'm coming straight, bang, up to Eastchester!"

"Come if you like, but you won't be admitted to this house. And I think you're acting horrid, Philip. Instead of being sorry for me, you just scold."

"I'm not scolding YOU, Patty, but I won't have you shut up there with that Cameron!"

"And Kenneth."

"Harper's all right, but that Cameron boy is too fresh, - and I don't want you to encourage him."

"All right, Philip, I won't encourage him. Good-bye." Patty spoke in her sweetest tones, and hung up the receiver suddenly, leaving Mr. Van Reypen in a state of mind bordering on frenzy.

Then Patty called up Nan, and explained the whole situation to her.

"How awful!" said Nan, in deepest sympathy, "both for Mrs. Perry and for you."

"Yes, it is; but of course there's nothing to do but make the best of it. Ken is splendid. If it weren't for his strength and courage I don't know how I'd bear it. But he won't let me give way. So I'm going to be a heroine and all that sort of thing, a real little Casablanca. Honestly, Nan, I feel ashamed of myself to think of my little bothers, - when the boys have their business matters to consider, and Mrs. Perry is in such deep trouble. So I'm going to do my best to be cheerful and pleasant. They say we may be here two or three weeks or more."

"Good gracious, Patty!"

"Yes, I know, - it's all of that! Now, Nan, I mustn't keep this telephone, for they all want to use it. But I'll call you up to-night or to-morrow, for a longer talk. I wish you'd send me up some clothes. Pack a suitcase or a steamer trunk with some little house-dresses and tea-gowns and lingerie, and send it along to-morrow. Then I'll tell you later what else I want. Tell father all about it, and ask him to call me up this evening. Good-bye for now."

Patty hung up the receiver, and Marie took her turn next.

"How did your people take it?" asked Cameron, as Patty came slowly back to the hall fireside, where they had all been sitting when the dreadful news was told.

"I told my mother," said Patty, "but I didn't give her a chance to say much. She was appalled, of course, at the whole business, but she's going to send me some clothes, and get along without me for a few weeks, - although I can't help feeling 'they will miss me at home, they will miss me.'"

Patty sang the line in a high falsetto that made them all laugh.

"Mother's about crazy!" announced Marie, as she came back from telephoning. "Not that she minds my staying here, but she's sure I'll have the diphtheria!"

"No, you won't, Marie," said Kit, earnestly. "I asked the doctor particularly, and he said there wasn't the least danger that any of us would develop the disease."

"Then why do we have to stay here?" asked Marie.

"Because the house is quarantined. By order of the Board of Health. You may as well make up your mind to it, cousin, and take it philosophically, as Miss Fairfield does."

Kenneth telephoned to his office, and then Kit shut himself up in the library and telephoned for a long time.

When he returned, he said, with an evident effort at cheerfulness, "Now let's pretend that we're not kept here against our will, but that this is a jolly house party. If we were here for a month, on invitation, we'd expect to have a bang-up time."

"But this is so different," said Patty, dolefully. "A house party would mean all kinds of gaiety and fun. But it doesn't seem right to be gay, when Babette is dangerously ill."

"But she isn't dangerously ill," said Kit, earnestly. "It may prove a very light case. But you see the quarantine laws are just as strict for a very light case as for a desperate one. Now, I propose that we try to forget Babette for the present, and go in for a good time."

"But we can't do anything," said Marie; "we can't go to places or have any company, or see anybody or write any letters -"

"There, there, little girl," said her cousin, "don't make matters worse by complaining. Here are four most attractive young people, in a perfectly lovely house, with all the comforts of home; and if we don't have a good time, it's our own fault. What shall we do this afternoon?"

"Let's play bridge," said Patty; "that's quiet, and I don't feel like anything rackety-packety."

"Bridge is good enough for me," said Kenneth, manfully striving to shake off the gloom he felt. He was really very much concerned about some important business matters, but he said nothing of this to any one.

They sat down at the bridge table, but the game dragged. No one seemed interested, and they dealt the cards in silence.

Cameron tried to keep up a lively flow of conversation, and the others tried to respond to his efforts. But though they succeeded fairly well, after the third rubber, Patty declared she could not play any longer, and she was going to her room for a nap.

"Come on," said Marie, jumping up, "I'll go with you."

"Yes, do, girlies," said Cameron, kindly. "A little nap will do you good. Come down for tea, won't you?"

"I don't know," said Patty, doubtfully; "I think we'll have tea in our rooms, and not come down till dinner time."

"As you like," returned Kit; "if we four have to live together for weeks, it won't do to see TOO much of each other!"

"Then perhaps we won't come down to dinner, either," said Patty, with a momentary flash of her roguish nature.

"Oh, you MUST!" exclaimed Kenneth, who couldn't help taking things seriously. "You two girls are the only bright spots in this whole business!"

"Thank you," and Patty smiled at him, as she and Marie went away.

"Come into my room," said Patty, "and let's talk this thing over."

Soon the two girls, in kimonos, were sitting either side of the cheerful wood fire, discussing the outlook.

"It's worse for you than for me, Patty," said Marie, "for you have more social engagements, and all that sort of thing, than I do. And besides, these are my relatives. But for you, almost a stranger, to be held up here like this, it's just awful! I can't tell you how bad I feel about it."

"Now, Marie, let up on that sort of talk! It's no more your fault than it is mine, and the fact of the Perrys being your relatives doesn't make a scrap of difference. To be honest, the thing nearly floored me at first, for I never had anything like this happen to me before. But that's all the more reason why I should brace up to this first occasion, - and from now on, you won't hear another peep of discontent out of ME. If we have to stay here four weeks or eight weeks or twelve weeks, I'm going to behave myself like a desirable citizen. And I'm only sorry that I've acted horrid so far."

"You haven't acted horrid, Patty."

"Yes, I have; when we played bridge I sat around like an old wet blanket. Now I'll tell you what, Marie, let's plan something nice for this evening. Something that will cheer up Mrs. Perry, and incidentally ourselves. But isn't it strange how we can't make it seem like a house party? Really, you know, it IS one, and Babette isn't sick enough, - at least, not yet, - for us to be gloomy and mournful. And yet, for the life of me, I can't feel gay and festive. But I'm going to MAKE myself feel so, if it takes all summer! We've two awfully nice boys to entertain us, and you and I are good congenial chums. Mrs. Perry is a dear and the baby is an awful comfort. Now why, Marie, WHY can't we act just as if there wasn't any Babette? I mean, of course, unless she gets very much worse."

"It isn't our concern for Babette that makes the trouble," said Marie, slowly; "it's our disappointment at our own inconvenience, and being kept here against our will."

"You clever little thing! You've put your finger right on the truth. You're right! Our anxiety for Babette is real enough as far as it goes, but it's secondary. The primary cause of our gloom IS pure selfishness! and the amazing part is, that I never realised it until you showed me! Now I have always thought that the sin I abhorred most was selfishness, and here I am giving way to it at the first opportunity. Well, it's got to stop! Now, then, let's plan something real nice and pleasant for this evening, and have a good time."

"I don't think anything would be nicer than music," said Marie. "Lora has a violin, and Kit and I will play, and you can sing -"

"And we'll all sing choruses and things, - real jolly ones, and enter into it with some spirit."

"Yes; Lora loves to have people sing, and she'll enjoy that."

"And then other nights," Patty went on, bravely, "we'll get up some entertainment. Tableaux, you know, or theatricals."

"Yes, and we can play games and things. Now shall we go down to tea?"

"No," and Patty wagged her head, sagely; "it's perfectly true that we mustn't give those boys too much of our delightful society or they won't appreciate it!

Let them wait for us till dinner time. We'll have our tea up here, and perhaps Mrs. Perry will be with us. Let the boys shift for themselves till dinner time, and then they'll be all the more glad to see us."

Nora brought the tea tray up to the girls, and with it a note.

"I thought they'd holler for us," said Patty, laughing as she read the note; "listen to this: 'Twin stars of light and joy, DO come down and illumine our dark and lonesome tea-table! We pine and languish without you! Oh, come QUICK, ere we fade away! Kit and Ken.' I thought they'd be lonesome," and Patty nodded her head, with a satisfied air. "Now you know, Marie, if we've got to take care of these boys for weeks, we must make them walk a chalk line."

"Yes, of course, Patty; shall we go down, or send a note?"

"Neither," returned Patty, with a toss of her head. "Nora, please say to the young gentlemen that the young ladies will be down at dinner time."

"Yes, Miss Fairfield," said Nora, departing.

A few moments later they heard the wailing strains of a violin, and listening at their door, heard Kit playing, with exaggerated effect. "Come into the Garden, Maud."

CHAPTER XII

A SURPRISE

"Good gracious, Marie!" exclaimed Patty, popping her head in at Marie's door, just before dinner time, "we haven't any clothes! Are you going to wear your party frock or the dress you wore up here?"

"'Deed I'm not going to put on my best gown for a little home dinner! The dresses we wore up here are all right. They're nice and pretty."

"But they're day frocks. I DO like to dress up for dinner."

"I'll help you out," said Lora Perry, who was present. "I've two or three trunkfuls of old-fashioned clothes, that ought to fit you girls fairly well. They're not antiques, you know; they're some I had before I was married, - but they're pretty. Go in the trunk room and rummage."

So the two girls went to inspect the frocks.

"Why, they're beautiful," said Patty; "I really think they're a lot prettier than the things we wear to-day. Oh, look at these big sleeves."

"Yes, leg o' mutton they used to call them."

"I know, but they're more the size of a side of beef! But these are street dresses. Where are the evening things?"

"Here are some," said Marie, opening another trunk.

"Oh, how lovely!" And Patty pounced on a white organdy, made with a full skirt and three narrow, lace-edged frills. There were wide, full petticoats to go with it, and Patty declared that was her costume. Marie found a dimity, of a Dresden-flowered pattern, with black velvet bows, which she appropriated, and they flew back to their rooms in triumph.

The white dress proved very becoming to Patty, and the square-cut neck of the bodice suited the lines of her pretty throat and shoulders. She wore a broad sash of blue ribbon and a knot of blue ribbon in her hair. Marie's dress was equally pretty, and they laughed heartily at the full, flaring skirts, so different from the narrow ones of their own wardrobe.

They went downstairs together, and found waiting for them two bored-looking young men, in immaculate evening clothes.

"Good-evening," said Patty, dropping a little curtsy; "SO glad to meet you."

"Thought you'd never come," returned Kit. "What are you, anyway? Masquerading as old-fashioned girls?"

"Are they old-fashioned togs?" said Kenneth. "I thought they looked different, but I didn't know what ailed them."

"They're perfectly beautiful evening frocks," Patty declared, "and you're not to make fun of them."

"Far be it from me to make fun of anything so charming," returned Cameron. "Come along, Captive Princess, dinner is waiting." He tucked Patty's hand in his arm, and as they walked to the dining-room, he murmured: "You really are a Captive Princess now, aren't you?"

"Yes, I am; and if you're my Knight, aren't you going to deliver me from durance vile?"

"Of course I am. I will be under your window at midnight with a rope ladder and a white palfrey."

"Well, if I'm awake I'll come down the ladder; but if not, don't expect me."

"But if you want to be rescued, you must take the opportunity when it offers."

"Oh, I'm not so sure I want to be rescued. I'm ready now to make the best of things and I'm planning to have a real good time while we stay here."

"Nice little Captive Princess! Nice little Princess Poppycheek! And am I included in these good times?"

"Yes, indeed. It will take the four of us; and Mrs. Perry, whenever we can get her, to have the good times I'm planning."

All through dinner time Patty was her own gay, merry

self. Babette was not mentioned, nor the fact that they were staying in Eastchester, under compulsion, and it might have been just a happy party invited there for pleasure.

Mr. Perry's absence was, of course, painfully noticeable. But Patty knew that Mrs. Peny had telephoned him all about the case, and she made no comment. She was determined that she would not be responsible for any allusion to their trouble.

After dinner Patty informed them all that a musicale would take place. Everybody agreed to this, and all joined in singing gay choruses and glees. Patty sang solos, and Kit and Marie played duets. Then Patty sang to a violin obligato, and altogether the concert was a real success.

"We ought to go on the road," said Kit, as he laid down his violin at last. "I think as a musical troupe we'd be a screaming success. Now, who's for a little dance to wind up with?"

"Do dance," said Mrs. Perry; "I'll play for you."

"Just one, then," said Patty, "for this is a rest-cure, you know; and I'm going to bed very early. Six weeks in the country is going to do wonders for me."

Though four weeks had been the extreme possibility of their stay, Patty whimsically kept calling it six weeks or eight weeks, because, as she said, that made four weeks seem less.

Cameron turned to Patty, as his sister began to play, and in a moment they were dancing.

"If we dance every night for twelve weeks," said Patty, "we ought to do fairly well together."

"When I think of that, I'm entirely reconciled to staying here," returned Kit. "Poppycheek, you are a wonderful dancer! You're like a butterfly skimming over a cobweb!"

"I don't dance a bit better than you do. You're almost like a professional, except that you're more graceful than they are."

"DON'T, Princess! don't talk to me like that, or I shall faint away from sheer delight! But as we both are such miraculous steppers, we might give exhibitions or something."

"Yes, or teach, and make our everlasting fortune."

"Well, I think we won't do either. We'll just reserve our glorious genius for our own enjoyment. Just think of dancing with you every night, for goodness knows how long!" said Kit.

"But you won't."

"Won't? Why not?"

"Because before we've been here many days we shall quarrel. I know we will. Four people can't be shut up inside four walls without quarrelling sooner or later."

"Well, let's make it later. And, anyway, I'm so good-natured, you couldn't quarrel with me if you tried."

"I couldn't quarrel with you while I'm dancing with

you, anyway. But now this dance is over and there's not to be another one to-night. Good-night, everybody. Come, Marie," and taking Marie by the hand, Patty led her upstairs at once.

"Oh, DON'T go!" cried the two young men, but Patty and Marie only leaned over the banisters, and called down laughing good-nights, and ran away to their rooms.

Next morning, Patty declared they must adhere to the policy of keeping more or less to themselves.

"I can put in a lovely morning," she said; "I shall visit the baby in the nursery and I shall read for awhile, and I'll have a long telephone conversation with Nan and perhaps some other people, and I'm not going downstairs till luncheon time. You do as you like, Marie."

Marie declared her intention of doing whatever Patty did, so the two girls spent a pleasant morning upstairs.

Mrs. Perry reported that Babette was no worse, and that the doctor had said nothing further than that.

At luncheon time, the girls went downstairs and were greeted with reproofs for being so late.

"We'll play with you this afternoon," said Patty, kindly, "but you can't expect to have our company all day. I've had a lovely time this morning; Baby Boo is an entertainment in herself."

"Why didn't you let me come up to the nursery?" said Kit. "That Kiddy-baby loves me."

"She does, indeed," said Patty, serenely; "she's been asking for Uncle Kit all the morning."

"Cruel Princess!" said Cameron; "you're not a bit nice to your Knight!"

"I'll make up for it this afternoon," and Patty flashed him a glance that seemed greatly to cheer him.

After lunch they all went into the library. Patty threw herself into a big arm-chair.

"Now, I want to be entertained," she said; "I'm perfectly amiable and affable and good-natured, but I wish to be amused. Will you do it, my Knight?"

"Ay, Princess, that will I!" and Cameron made a flourishing and obsequious bow before her. "Would it amuse your Royal Highness to learn that you're going home this afternoon?"

"That is but a cruel jest," said Patty, "and so, not amusing. If it were the truth, it would be good hearing, indeed."

"But it IS the truth, fair lady." Cameron looked at his watch. "In about an hour, the speedy motor will convey us all back to the busy mart and to our homes."

"What do you mean?" cried Patty, starting up; for she saw that it was not a mere jest.

"May I make a speech?" and Cameron took the middle of the floor, while his hearers sat in breathless silence.

Mrs. Perry had a twinkle in her eye, Kenneth looked

hopeful, but the girls' faces expressed only blank wonder.

"To begin with," said Mr. Cameron, in a cool, even voice, "we're not quarantined, and never have been. To proceed, Babette has not the diphtheria, and never has had. In a word, and I trust I shall not be flayed alive, - this whole affair is a practical joke, which I have had the honour to perpetrate on Miss Patricia Fairfield, and for which I claim the payment of a wager made by the fair lady herself!"

Patty's blue eyes stared at him. At first, a furious wave of anger swept over her, and then her sense of justice made her realise that she had no right to be angry. It took her a few moments to realise the whole situation, and then she began to laugh.

She jumped up and went to Cameron, and with her little fist she pounded his broad shoulder.

"*I* - THINK - YOU'RE - PERFECTLY - HORRID!!" she exclaimed, emphasising each word by a pound on his shoulders.

Then she stood back with dignity. "How DARE you do such a thing?" she cried, stamping her foot at him.

"There, there, little Princess, - little Captive Princess, - don't take it so hard! Don't let your joy at your escape be marred by your chagrin at having been caught!"

"Do you mean to say, Cameron," said Kenneth, rather sternly, "that you trumped up this quarantine business, and it's all a fake?"

"Just exactly that," said Cameron, calmly, and looking Ken steadily in the eye.

"You've made me a lot of trouble, old man," and Kenneth's voice was regretful rather than reproachful.

"Oh, not so much," said Cameron, airily. "I took the liberty of telephoning your office after you did yesterday, and told them that it was probable you'd be back there this afternoon."

Kenneth stared at him speechlessly, stupefied by this exhibition of nerve.

"Did you know all about it, Lora?" demanded Marie, turning to Mrs. Perry.

"Yes," said that lady, between spasms of laughter. "I didn't want to do it, but Kit just made me! You see, Babette did have an awful sore throat, and we did call a nurse, but the doctor said, that while it might turn toward diphtheria, there was small danger of it. And, this morning, he said even that danger had passed. Truly, girls, I didn't consent willingly, but Kit coaxed me into it. Of course, I telephoned Dick the whole story, and he stayed in town last night, but he's coming home this afternoon. You're not angry, are you, Patty?"

"I don't know whether I am or not. I'm a little bewildered as yet. But I think, in fairness, I shall have to admit it was a most successful practical joke, - as such jokes go."

"And it fulfilled all your conditions?" asked Cameron, eagerly.

"I'm not sure of that. We agreed that it must be clever and not unkind. It was certainly clever, but wasn't it a little unkind to cause trouble to so many people? Mrs. Homer, for instance?"

"No!" exclaimed Kit, hastily. "I telephoned last evening to auntie, and told her that there was probability that the quarantine would be lifted to-day. I telephoned the same thing to Mrs. Fairfield, but I told both ladies not to mention that to you girls, as I didn't want to raise false hopes. Oh, I looked out for every point, and you're not angry with me, are you, Princess?"

He was so wheedlesome and so boyish in his enjoy-ment of the joke, that Patty hadn't the heart to scold him, nor was she sure she had any reason to do so.

"I admit it," she said, "you certainly did play a practical joke on me successfully, though I didn't think you could. You have won the wager, and I shall of course pay my debt. But just now, I'm interested in the fact that we're going home. And yet," she added, turning to her hostess, "isn't it funny? Now that we CAN go, I don't want to go! Now it seems like a house party again."

Patty beamed around on them all, and seemed a different girl from the Patty of the last twenty-four hours.

"You were a brick!" said Kenneth, "through it all. I know how you suffered, but you bravely forgot yourself in trying to make it pleasant for the others."

"Nonsense! I acted like a pig! A horrid, round, fat pig!

But, truly, it was the most different sensation to be quarantined here or to be visiting here. I wouldn't believe, if I hadn't tried it, what a difference there is! Oh, it's just lovely here, now!" and Patty executed a little fancy dance, singing a merry little song to it.

"Well, I'll tell you how to get even," said Mrs. Perry; "all of you come up here again soon, for a little visit, and leave Kit at home! Then I guess he'll be sorry."

At this, Kit emitted a wail of grief and anguish, and then the girls ran away to pack their things for the homeward trip.

Within the hour, they had started for New York. Patty had entirely forgiven Cameron, and was ready to enjoy the memory of the affair as a good joke upon herself.

"I don't approve of practical jokes," she said, by way of summing up. "I never did, and I don't now. But I know that I brought it on myself by making that foolish bet, and it has taught me a lesson never to do such a thing again. And I forgive you, Mr. Kit Cameron, only on condition that you give me your promise never to play a joke on me again. I admit that you CAN do it, but I ask that you WON'T do it."

"I promise, Princess," said Cameron. "Henceforward, there shall be no jokes between us, - of course, I mean practical jokes. But you will make good your wager?"

"Certainly; I always pay my just debts."

"May I come and collect the debt this evening?"

" No , that's too soon; come to-morrow night, if you

like. This evening I devote to a reunion with my family."

"Nobody else?"

"Possibly somebody else, - somebody who was defrauded by your precious joke." And then a sudden light dawned upon Patty. "WAS your quarantine idea worked up in order to keep me away from New York last night?"

"Partly," said Cameron, honestly; "I didn't see any other way to cut out Van Reypen, and it fitted in with my whole plan, so why not?"

"It wasn't very nice of you."

"All's fair in love and war," and Cameron laughed so gaily, that Patty concluded it was wiser to drop the subject.

"*I* think it was awfully hard for poor Mr. Van Reypen to lose Patty from the party, because of your old joke!" exclaimed Marie.

"I don't mind that part of it," said Kenneth; "he might as well have a little corner of the joke, as the rest of us. But if I've lost a five thousand dollar deal on this, I'll sue you for damages, Cameron."

"Sue ahead," said the irrepressible Kit; "I've danced, and I'm willing to pay the piper."

Kenneth and Marie were left at their homes, and the car went on to Patty's house.

"May I come in?" said Cameron, as they reached it.

"No, indeed!" said Patty, and then she added, "I don't know - yes - perhaps you'd better. If father storms about this thing, I think you ought to be there and face the music."

"I think so, too," said Cameron, with alacrity; "I'd rather be there, and help my little Princess weather the storm."

They found Mr. and Mrs. Fairfield both at home, and they created an immense surprise by suddenly appearing before them.

"Why, Patty Fairfield!" cried Nan, "you DEAR child!" She wrapped Patty in her embrace as if welcoming one long lost. Nor was Mr. Fairfield less fervent in his demonstrations of welcome.

They shook Cameron warmly by the hand, and Nan rang for tea and said: "Tell us all about it! How did you get out? Was it a false alarm? Wasn't it diphtheria? Oh, Mr. Cameron, you relieved us so greatly last night, when you told us it might be a mistaken diagnosis! What is the matter with you two? What are you giggling about?"

And then the whole story came out. Cameron and Patty both talked at once, Cameron making a clean breast of the matter, and assuming all the blame, while Patty made excuses for him, and offered conciliatory explanations.

Nan went off in peals of laughter and declared it was the best joke she had ever heard.

But Mr. Fairfield hesitated as to his verdict. He asked many questions, to which he received straightforward answers.

At last, he said: "It was a prank, and I cannot say I think it was an admirable performance. But young folks will be young folks, and I trust I'm not so old and grouty as to frown on innocent fun. To my mind, this came perilously near NOT being entirely innocent, but I'm not going to split hairs about it. I don't care for such jokes myself, but I must admit, Cameron, you played it pretty cleverly. And you certainly did your share toward lessening any anxieties that might have been caused to other people. So there's my hand on it, boy, but if you'll take an older man's advice, put away these childish pranks as you take on the dignity of years."

"Thank you, Mr. Fairfield," said Cameron, "you make me feel almost ashamed of myself; but, truly, sir, I am addicted to jokes. I can't seem to help it!"

The handsome face was so waggish and full of sheer, joyous fun, that they all laughed and the matter was amicably settled.

"But I want my picture," Cameron said, as he rose to go.

"And you shall have it," said Patty, running out of the room.

She returned with a cabinet photograph, wrapped in a bit of tissue paper.

" Please appreciate it," she said, demurely, "for never

before have I given my photograph to a young man. They say it is an excellent likeness of me."

Cameron removed the paper, and saw a picture of Patty taken at the age of two years.

It was a lovely baby picture, with merry eyes and smiling lips.

The quick-witted young man betrayed none of the disappointment he felt, and only said, "It is indeed a striking likeness! I never saw a better photograph! Thank you, a thousand times."

Then, amid the general laughter that ensued, Cameron went away.

The Fairfields discussed the whole matter, and Patty finally summed up the consensus of opinion, by saying: "Well, I don't care! It was an awfully good joke, and he's an awfully nice boy!"

CHAPTER XIII

SISTER BEE

One afternoon Patty and Marie Homer were coming home from a concert.

Patty had grown very fond of Marie. They were congenial in many ways, and especially so in their love of music, and often went together to concerts or recitals.

It was late in March, but as spring had come early the afternoon was warm and Marie proposed, as the two girls got into the Homer limousine, that they go for a ride through the park.

"A short one, then," said Patty, "for I must be home fairly early!"

"Then don't let's go in the park," said Marie, "let's go to my house, instead. For I want you to meet Bee. She's just home for her Easter vacation."

"I can only stay a minute; but I will go. I do want to see Bee. How long will she be at home?"

"More than a fortnight. She has quite a holiday. Oh, there'll be gay doings while Bee's at home. She keeps the house lively with her pranks, and if she and Kit get started they're sure to raise mischief."

"How old is Beatrice?"

"She's just seventeen, but sometimes she acts like a kiddy of twelve. Mother says she doesn't know what to do with her, the child is so full of capers."

As the two girls entered the Homer apartment, Beatrice Homer ran to meet them.

"Oh, you're Patty Fairfield! I KNOW you are! Aren't you the loveliest thing ever! You look like a bisque ornament to set on a mantel-piece. Are you real?"

She poked her finger in Patty's dimpled cheek, but she was so roguish and playful, that Patty could not feel annoyed with her.

"Let me look at you," Patty said, holding her off, "and see what YOU'RE like. Why, you're a gipsy, an elfin sprite, a witch of the woods! You have no business to be named Beatrice."

"I know it," said Bee, dancing around on her toes. "But my nickname isn't so bad for me, is it?" And she waved her arms and hovered around Patty, making a buzzing noise like a real bee.

"Don't sting me!" cried Patty.

"Oh, I don't sting my friends! I'm a honey-bee. A dear, little, busy, buzzy honey-bee!" And she kept on dancing around and buzzing till Patty put out her hand as if to brush her away.

"Buzz away, Bee, but get a little farther off, - you drive me distracted."

"That's the way she always acts," said Marie, with a sigh; "we can't do anything with her! It's a pity she was ever nicknamed Bee, for, when she begins buzzing, she's a regular nuisance."

"Sometimes I'm a drone," Bee announced, and with that she began a droning sound that was worse than the buzzing, and kept it up till it set their nerves on edge.

"Oh, Bee, dear!" Marie begged of her, "WON'T you stop that and be nice?"

Bee's only answer was a long humming drone.

Patty looked at the girl kindly. "I want to like you," she said, "and I think it's unkind of you not to let me do it."

Bee stopped her droning and considered a moment. Then she smiled, and when her elfin face broke into laughter, she was a pretty picture, indeed.

"I DO want you to like me," she said, impulsively, grasping Patty's hands; "and I will be good. You know I'm like the little girl, - the curly girlie, you know, - when she was good she was awful drefful good, and when she was bad she was horrid."

"I'm sure you couldn't be horrid," and Patty smiled at her, "but all the same I don't believe you can be very, VERY good."

"Oh, yes, I can; the goodest thing you ever saw! Now watch me," and sure enough during the rest of Patty's stay, Beatrice was as charming and delightful a companion as any one you'd wish to see. She was bubbling over with fun and merriment, but she refrained from teasing, and Patty took a decided liking to her.

"I'll make a party for you, Bee," she said. "What kind would you like?"

"Not a stiff, stuck-up party. I hate 'em. Can't it be a woodsy kind of a thing?"

"A ramble through the park?"

"More woodsy than that. The park is almost like the city."

"Well, a picnic to Bronx Park, then, or Van Cortlandt."

"That sounds better. But I'll come to any party you make, - I know it will be lovely. Oh, I'll tell you, Patty, what I'd like best. To go on one of your Saturday after-noon jinks; with the queer, poor people, you know."

"They're not queer and they're not always very poor," returned Patty, seriously; "I'm afraid you'd tease them or make fun of them."

"Honest Injun, I wouldn't! Please let me go, and I'll be heavenly nice to them. They'll simply adore me! Please, pretty Patty!"

"Of course I will, since you've promised to be nice to them."

"Oh, you lovely Patty! Don't you sometimes get tired

of being so pink and white?"

"Of course I do. I wish I could be brown and dark-eyed like you."

"You'd soon wish yourself back again. Can't you combine the woodsy party and the Happy Chaps, or whatever you call them?"

"I think we can," smiled Patty, who had already planned a Saturday afternoon picnic, and would be glad to include Bee.

"But Bee has to learn to behave properly at formal parties," said Marie. "I'm going to give a luncheon for her, while she's at home, and it's going to be entirely grown-up and conventional."

"Don't want it!" and Bee scowled darkly.

"That doesn't matter. Mother says we must have it, and that you must behave properly. You have to learn these things, you know."

"Oh, Bee will do just exactly right, I know," said Patty, as she rose to go. "If she doesn't, we can't let her come to the picnic. When is the luncheon, Marie?"

"We haven't quite decided yet, but I must send out the invitations in a day or two."

Patty went home, thinking about this sister of Marie's.

"She's an awfully attractive little piece," she said to Nan, later, "but you never can tell what she's going to do next. I think if she had the right training, she'd be a lovely girl, but Mrs. Homer and Marie spoil her with indulgence and then suddenly scold her for her unconventionality. Perhaps the school she's attending will bring her out all right, but she's a funny combination of naughty child and charming girl. She would stop at nothing, and I don't wonder that they say when she and Kit Cameron get together, look out for breakers."

A few days later, Patty received an invitation to Marie's luncheon for her sister.

It was formally written, and the date set was Tuesday, April the eighth, at half-past one. Patty noted the day on her engagement calendar, and thought no more about it at the time. But a day or two later it suddenly occurred to her that she had heard that Beatrice was to return to school on the seventh of April.

"I must be mistaken about her going back," Patty thought, remembering the luncheon on the eighth, and then, lest she herself might be mistaken in the date, she looked at the invitation again. It read "the eighth," and though Marie's handwriting was scrawly and not very legible, the figure eight was large and plain.

"She ought to have spelled it out," said Patty, who was punctilious in such matters.

"Yes," agreed Nan, "it's those little details that count so much among society people."

"Well, the Homers are dears, but they lack just that little something that makes people know when to spell their figures and when not to. I think it's horrid when people spell a date in ordinary correspondence. But an invitation is another thing. But I say, Nan, - Jiminetty crickets!"

"I'm not sure that date-spelling people ought to refer to those crickets," said Nan, lifting her eyebrows.

"Well, Jerusalem crickets, then! and every kind of crickets in the ornithology or whatever they belong in. But, Nan, I've discovered something!"

"What, Miss Columbus?"

"Oh, I'm a Sherlock Holmes! I'm Mr. D. Tective! What DO you think?"

"If you really want to know, I think you're crazy! jumping around like a wild Indian, and you a this season's debutante!"

"Rubbish! most debutantes are wild Indians at times. But, Nan, I've discovered their secret! Hah! the vilyuns! but they shall be foiled! foiled!! FOILED!!!"

Patty raged up and down the room, melodramatically clutching at her hair and staring at Nan with her blue eyes. "It is a deep-laid plot, but it shall be foiled by Patricia Sherlock, - the only lady detective in captivity!"

"Patty, do behave yourself! What is the matter with you? You act like a lunatic!"

"I'll tell you, Nan, honey," and Patty suddenly sat down on the couch, among a pile of pillows. "But first read that invitation and see if you see anything unusual or suspicious about it."

"I can hardly read it; for this writing looks like that on the obelisk, - or at least it's nearly as unintelligible. But it seems to say that Mrs. Robert Homer requests the pleasure of your company at luncheon on Tuesday, April the eighth, at half-past one o'clock. Nothing criminal about that, is there?"

"Is there! There is, indeed! Nan, you're the dearest, sweetest, loveliest lady in the whole world, but you can't see a hole through a ladder. So I'll tell you. The date of that party is really April the FIRST. I mean, Marie wrote April the first! And if you'll observe, somebody else has put a twisty line around that ONE and made it into an EIGHT! Why, it's as plain as day!"

"It certainly is, Patty," and Nan looked at the girl in astonishment and admiration. "How did you ever happen to notice it?"

"Why, it just jumped out at me. See, a different pen was used. The line is thicker. And nobody would make an EIGHT that way. They'd make it all with one pen mark. And this is a straight up-and-down ONE, and that rest of it was put on later. And, anyway, Nan, if there were any doubt, don't you see it isn't TH after it as it ought to be for the eight, it's ST?"

"You can't tell which it is in this crazy handwriting," and Nan scrutinised the page.

"Yes, you can," and Patty stared at it. "You wouldn't notice the difference, if you weren't looking for it, but it IS ST. I see it all, Nan! You know Bee didn't want this luncheon, and to get out of it, she changed that date before the invitations were sent! And you see, by the eighth, she'll be back in school!"

"Are both dates Tuesday?" said Nan, thinking.

"Yes, of course, they are. Isn't it clever? Oh, Bee never got this up all by herself, - that Kit helped her."

"But, Patty, then nobody will go on the first, and the Homers will be all prepared -"

"That's just what Bee wants! One of her practical jokes! Oh, Nan, I do detest practical jokes."

"So do I! I think they're ill-bred."

"But the Homers don't think that, and Kit Cameron doesn't, either. We've discussed that matter lots of times, and we never agree. And, besides, Nan," and Patty had a new inspiration, "don't you see, this party was planned for the first of April, and Bee and Kit will call this thing an April Fool joke, and therefore entirely permissible. April Fool's Day is their Happy Hunting Ground. But I'm going to foil this thing, and don't you forget it! Seems to me it would be a pretty good joke if I'd turn the tables on those two smarties."

"How can you, Patty?"

"I haven't quite thought it out yet, but I have an idea."

"But, Patty, wait a minute. Perhaps they only changed the date on yours, - just to fool you, you know."

"Good gracious, Nan! perhaps that's so! How did you come to think of it? But I'll soon find out."

Patty flew to the telephone, and in a short time learned that both Mona and Elise were invited for the eighth, and she concluded that the plotters had changed the date on all the invitations.

Next she called up Marie, and without letting her know why, asked for a list of the luncheon guests.

Marie told her at once, without asking why she wanted to know.

There were nine beside the Homers, and Patty was acquainted with them all.

She called them up each in turn on the telephone, and explained carefully that a mistake had been made in the invitations, and she hoped they would come on the first instead of the eighth.

Fortunately, all of them were able to do this, and Patty enjoined each one to say nothing about this change of date, until they should arrive at the party.

To a few of her more intimate friends, - Mona, Elise, and Christine,-she told the whole story, and they fell in with her plans.

And so it came about, that on the first of April preparations were going blithely forward in the Homer apartment, for Bee's elaborate luncheon.

It was all true, exactly as Patty had figured it out; and Kit and Beatrice had planned what they considered a first-class and entirely permissible practical joke.

They knew that Mrs. Homer would make elaborate preparations for the luncheon, but they agreed that there would be no other harm done. And to them, the fun of seeing the perplexity of Marie and her mother at the non-appearance of their guests, was sufficient reason for their scheme. Moreover, they fell back on the time-honoured tradition that any joke was justifiable on April Fools' Day.

In addition to all this, Beatrice did not want to attend the luncheon party, and as by chance it had been left to her to seal up and address the invitations that Marie had written, and as Kit came in while she was doing it, their fertile brains had discovered that, as the dates fell on the same day of the week, the first could easily be changed to the eighth! And the two sinners chuckled with glee over the fact that another luncheon would have to be prepared the week following.

As it neared one o'clock on the first of April, Kit strolled into the Homers' apartment.

"Run away, little boy," said his aunt, gaily; "we're having a young ladies' party here to-day, and you're not invited."

"Please let me stay a little while, auntie; I'll run away before your guests arrive. Mayn't I help you fix flowers or something?"

"No, you're more bother than help; now be good, Kit boy, and run away."

"Auntie," and Kit put on his most wheedlesome smile, which was always compelling, "if you'll just let me stay till the first guest comes, I'll scoot out at once."

Bee nearly choked at this, for did she not know that the guests wouldn't arrive for a week yet!

Mrs. Homer was called away to the dining-room then, and the two conspirators indulged in a silent dance of triumph over the success of their scheme. Not for a moment did it strike them as unkind or mean, because they had been used to practical jokes all their life, and this seemed to them the biggest and best they had ever carried off.

At half-past one Patty appeared.

She had laid her plans most carefully, and everything was going smoothly.

Mrs. Homer and Marie greeted her warmly, and Beatrice and Kit were not much surprised to see her, because she was liable to come any day. Beatrice looked a little surprised at Patty's dressed-up appearance, but as no one else appeared, she had no suspicion of what Patty had done.

They all sat in the drawing-room, and the clock ticked away until twenty-five minutes of two, but nobody else arrived.

Mrs. Homer grew restless. She looked at the clock, and turning to Kit, asked him if the time was right by his watch.

"Yes, auntie," replied that scapegrace. "It's almost twenty minutes of two. I thought you invited your friends for one-thirty."

"I did," and Mrs. Homer looked anxious. "How strange that no one is here, except Patty!"

Patty said nothing, but the enigmatic smile which she

cast on Kit made him feel that perhaps she knew more than she was telling.

"Do run away, Kit," urged his aunt. "I should think you'd be ashamed to come to a party where you're not invited."

"Perhaps I shall be invited if I wait long enough," and Kit threw a meaning glance at Beatrice. "If your guests don't come, auntie, you'll be glad to have me to help eat up your goodies."

"Not come! Of course they'll come!" cried Mrs. Homer, and Marie turned pale with dismay.

"Well, it seems to me," went on Kit, "that it would be a jolly good April Fool joke on you all, if they didn't come. And" - he rolled his eyes toward the ceiling, - "something tells me that they won't."

"What!" And Marie jumped up, her eyes blazing. Kit's roguish chuckle and Bee's elfin grin made Marie suddenly realise there was something in the air.

But before Kit could reply, Patty rose, and said directly to him, "How strange! I wonder what it is that tells you the luncheon guests won't come. How do you know?" - and she smiled straight at him. "Something tells ME that they WILL come!"

Then Patty herself stepped into the hall, threw open the door, and in came eight merry, laughing girls!

Patty had arranged that Elise should stay downstairs and receive each guest, and keep them there until all had arrived. Then they were to come upstairs, and wait outside the Homers' door, until the dramatic moment.

Although not in favour of practical jokes, Patty couldn't help enjoying Kit's absolutely paralysed face. He looked crestfallen, - but more than that, he looked so bewildered and utterly taken back, that Patty burst into laughter.

CHAPTER XIV

KENNETH

Mrs. Homer and Marie were greeting the newcomers, and as yet had hardly realised the whole situation, but quick-witted Beatrice took it all in.

"You Patty!" she cried, "oh, you Patty Fairfield!"

Patty's beaming face left no doubts as to who it was that had circumvented their plan and carried off the honours of the day.

"I'm so sorry you can't stay to luncheon," she said, turning to Kit; "must you really go now?"

"You little rascal!" he cried, "but I'll get even with you for this!"

"Please don't," and Patty spoke seriously. "Truly, Kit, I don't like these things. I'm awfully glad I could save Mrs. Homer and Marie the mortification and annoyance you and Bee had planned for them. But I haven't any right to talk to you like a Dutch aunt. If this is your notion of fun, I've no right even to criticise it; but I will tell you that if you 'get even with me,' as you call it, by playing one of your jokes on me, we'll not be friends any more."

"Patty!" and Kit took both her hands with a mock tragic gesture, "ANYTHING but that! To lose your friendship, Poppycheek, would be to lose all that makes life worth living! Now, if I promise to get even with you, by never trying to get even with you, - how's that?"

"That's just right!" and Patty, as the victorious party, could afford to be generous. "Now run away, Kit. You promised your aunt you'd scoot when her guests arrived."

"Yes, I did, Princess, so off I go! I haven't told you yet what I think of your cleverness in this matter, - by the way, how did you get on to it?"

"I'll tell you some other time; run away, now."

So Kit went away, and Patty turned back to the laughing group who were merrily discussing the joke.

Mrs. Homer and Marie were so horrified when they learned of their narrow escape from trouble, and so gratified that through Patty it had been an escape, that their feelings were decidedly mixed.

Beatrice was by nature what is called a good loser, and she took her defeat gaily.

"I had thought," she said, "that Kit and I were the best practical jokers in the world; but we've been beaten by Patty Fairfield! Now, that you're all here, I'm really glad of it, but I did think it would be fun to see mother and Marie hopping around, waiting for you!"

Then they all went out to luncheon, and among the

pretty table decorations and merry first of April jests, Patty managed to smuggle in at Bee's place a funny little figure. It was a bauble doll dressed like a Jester or Court Fool. And he bore a tiny flag in his hand, bearing the legend, April first.

"I AM an April Fool!" Beatrice admitted, as she took her seat, "but I forgive Patty for making me one, if all of the rest of you will forgive me."

Bee made this apology so prettily, and her roguish dark eyes flashed so brightly, that forgiveness was freely bestowed, and indeed, as one of the guests remarked, there was nothing to forgive.

But the story was told over and over again, and Patty was beset with questions as to how she chanced to discover the fraud.

"Why, I just happened to," she said, smiling; "I think I'm a detective by instinct; but there's not much credit due to me, for I knew Beatrice and Mr. Cameron were always planning jokes, and I couldn't believe they'd let the first of April pass by without some special demonstration. So I kept my eyes open, - and I couldn't help seeing what I did see."

"You're a Seer from Seeville," declared Bee, "and I promise I shall never try to trick you again."

"Which means," said Patty, calmly, "that you'll never cease trying until you accomplish it, and you say that to put me off my guard."

The baffled look on Bee's face proved that this was true, and everybody laughed.

It was that very same evening that Kenneth came to call, and Patty merrily told him the whole story.

She was not much surprised that he disapproved heartily of the joke.

"It isn't nice, Patty," he declared; "I may be dull and serious-minded, but I can't stand for jokes of that sort."

"I either, Ken," Patty returned; "but we must remember that people in this world have different ideas and tastes. And especially, they have differing notions of what constitutes humour. So, just because WE don't like practical jokes, we oughtn't to condemn those who do. We may like some things that THEY don't approve."

"What a just little person you are, Patty," and Harper looked at her approvingly. "For all your gaiety and frivolity you have a sound, sweet nature. And more than that, you have real brains in that curly-pate of yours."

"Goodness, Ken, you overwhelm me with these sudden compliments! You'll quite turn my head; I never COULD stand flattery!"

"It isn't flattery," and Kenneth spoke very earnestly; "it's the solemn truth. You are as wise and sensible as you are beautiful."

"Heavens and earth! Ken, WHY these kind words? What do you want?"

Harper looked at her a moment, and then said, steadily: "I want YOU, Patty; I want you more than I can tell you. I didn't mean to blurt this out so soon, but I can't keep it back. Patty, PATTY, can't you care for me a little?"

Patty was about to reply flippantly, but the look in Harper's eyes forbade it, and she said, gently, "Kenneth, dear, PLEASE don't!"

"I know what that means; it means you DON'T care."

"But I DO, Ken -"

"Oh, Patty, DO you? Do you MEAN it?"

Kenneth took her hands in his and his big grey eyes expressed so much love and hope, that Patty was frightened.

"No, I DON'T mean it! I don't mean anything! Oh, Ken, please DON'T!"

"Don't say that, Patty, because I MUST. Listen, dear; I went to see your father to-day. And I asked him if I might tell you all this."

Patty looked at him, not quite comprehending.

"You went to see daddy?" she said, wonderingly; "he never told me."

"Why should he? Don't you understand, dear? I went to him to ask his permission to tell you that I love you, and I want you for my wife. And your father said that I might tell you. And now, - darling -"

"And now it's up to me?" Patty tried to speak lightly.

"Exactly that, Patty," and Kenneth's face was grave and tender. "It's up to you, dear. The happiness of my whole life is up to you,-here and now. What's the answer?"

Patty sat still a moment, and fairly blinked her eyes in her endeavour to realise the situation.

"Ken," she said at last, in a small, far-away voice, "are you - are you - are you proposing to me?"

"I sure am!" and Kenneth's head nodded a firm assent; "the sooner you get that fact into your head, the better. Patty, DEAR little Patty, tell me, - don't keep me waiting -"

"But, Ken, I don't WANT to be proposed to, - and least of all, by YOU!"

"Patty, do you mean that?" and Harper's strained, anxious face took on a look of despair.

"Oh, no, NO, I don't mean THAT! At least, not in the way you think! I only mean we've been such good friends for so long, you're the last one I should think of marrying!"

"And who is the first one you think of marrying?"

Patty burst into laughter. "Oh, Ken, you're so funny when you're sarcastic! Don't be THAT, whatever you are!"

" I won't; Patty, darling, tell me you love me a little bit, - or just that you'll let me love you, - and I'll NEVER be sarcastic! I'll only be tender, and gentle, and loving, - and anything and everything you want me to be!"

"Can you?"

The eager light faded from Kenneth's eyes, as he answered: "No, I'm afraid I can't, dear. I know as well as you do, that I haven't the kind of gaiety you like in a man. I've told you this before. But, Patty, - you've so much of that, - don't you think you've enough for two?"

Patty smiled. "It isn't only that, Ken. Don't think that I care more for foolish, witty speeches than I do for a true, noble heart, like yours."

"DON'T say 'true, noble heart'! It sounds as if you didn't care two cents for me! But my heart, Patty, such as it is, is all yours, and has been ever since Vernondale days. Have you forgotten those?"

"No, indeed, and that's just what I say, Ken, we've been friends from the first, - and we're friends now."

"But the time has come, Patty, to be more than friends. I have known it a long time. And I want you to know it too, dear. Patty, - can't you?"

And then, all of a sudden, Patty KNEW she couldn't. Like a flash, she saw Kenneth just as he was, a strong, brave, true man, for whom she felt a warm friendship, but whom she knew she never could love. She might some time perhaps, in days to come, love somebody, but it would never, never be Kenneth Harper.

The thought made her sad, not for herself, but she

hated to give pain to this kind, honest man. She realised the depth of his love for her, and it broke her heart that she could not return it.

"Kenneth," she began, "I can't love you the way you want me to, - I just can't. And, anyway, I'm too young to think about these things."

"No, you're not, Patty. You're almost twenty and I'm twenty-four. That isn't too young, - it's just exactly the right age for lovers. It isn't too young, Patty, - if you love me."

"But I don't, Ken. I'm sorry, - but I don't."

"But you will. Oh, Patty, say you will try to!"

"Kenneth, does love come by trying?" and Patty looked into Kenneth's face, with a wide-eyed, serious gaze.

"I don't know why it shouldn't. Take time, dearest, to think about it, if you want to, but don't say no, irrevocably."

"Is a woman's no ever irrevocable?" And a smile dimpled Patty's face.

"Oh, Patty, you are so sweet when you smile like that! Please say you'll think about it."

"It won't do any good to think about it, Ken. If ever I marry anybody, it'll be somebody that I know I'm in love with, without thinking about it."

"There isn't anybody, is there, Patty, that you know

Carolyn Wells

you're in love with?"

"No, there isn't," and Patty's honest eyes showed that she spoke the truth. "But I'll tell you what, Ken, YOU try to like somebody else. Marie Homer is perfectly lovely! or, - there is Elise -"

"Hush, Patty, you don't know what you're talking about. I'm in love with you, - and you needn't suggest other girls to me."

"They're a great deal nicer than I am," said Patty, thoughtfully.

"Rubbish! You're the only girl in the world for me, and I want YOU. Are you sure there's nobody you like better than me, Patty?"

Patty rested her dimpled chin on the backs of her clasped hands and seemed to ponder this question. At last she said: "There's nobody I like better than you, Ken; but I've counted up nine, that I like just exactly as well. Now, what would you do in a case like that?"

"Patty, you're a torment! But if I have an even chance with the others, I shall get ahead, somehow. Are you sure you don't like that Cameron chap any better than me?"

"Not a bit better. He's good fun, but I can't imagine anybody falling in love with him."

"And - Van Reypen?"

The pink in Patty's cheeks deepened, and the lids fell over her blue eyes at this question. Af-ter an instant's pause, she said: "I don't think it's fair, Ken, for you to quiz me like that. And, anyway, I can't tell. In some ways, I like you a heap better than Phil Van Reypen, - and then in other ways -"

"You like him a heap better than me!" Kenneth's tone was accusing, and Patty resented it.

"Yes, I do!" she said, honestly. "He's always ready for a good time and willing to give up things for other people. Why, Ken, when you've an important case on, you won't go skating or anything! I have to coax you to come to my parties. Now, Phil is always ready to go anywhere or do anything."

"But he's a millionaire, Patty. He doesn't have to grub for a living, as I do."

"It isn't that, Ken." Patty's quick perceptions had caught the flaw in Kenneth's argument. "It isn't that. It's because you're so absorbed in your work that you'd RATHER dig and delve in it, than to go to parties. That's all right, of course, and much to your credit. But you can't blame me for liking a man who is willing to throw over his business engagements for me."

"That's just like you, Patty, to see through me so quickly. You're right. I don't care an awful lot for society doings. I only go to parties and things to see you. And it's mighty little satisfaction, for you're always so surrounded by rattle-pated men, that there's no getting near you."

"Wait a minute, Ken; is it fair to call them rattle-pated, when you only mean that they enjoy the kind of gay chatter that you look down upon?"

"Oh, Patty, I do love you so! And when you say things like that, that proves what a big, clear mind you have underneath your frivolity, I love you more than ever. Of course, as you saw at once, I call them rattle-pates out of sheer envy and jealousy, because they possess that quality we're speaking of, and I don't. Teach it to me, Patty; teach me to be a gay society man, dancing attendance on gay society girls –"

Patty burst into a peal of laughter at this notion of Kenneth's.

"I could do that, Ken, about as easily as you could teach me to be a quiet, demure, little person like Christine Hepworth. This is Christine:"

Patty sat upright with her hands clasped in her lap, and drew down the corners of her mouth, and rolled her eyes upward with a saint-like expression.

Then, "This is me!" she said. And jumping up, she pirouetted, whirling, around the room, waving her arms like a graceful butterfly skimming over flowers. Faster and faster she went, seeming scarcely to touch the tips of her toes to the floor, and smiling at Kenneth like a tantalising fairy.

Harper gazed at her, fascinated, and then as she hovered near him, jumped up, and caught her in his arms.

"You beauty!" he cried, but Patty slipped away from him.

"You haven't caught me yet, Ken," she said, laughing, "not for keeps, you know." The rollicking dance had restored her gaiety, and relieved the seriousness of the situation.

"You know perfectly well," she went on, standing across the room from him, and shaking a little pink forefinger at him, "you know perfectly well, Kenneth-boy, that we're not a bit suited to each other. I go through life the way I just flew around the room; and you go this way:" Patty dropped her arms at her side and marched stiffly around the room with a military air, gazing straight ahead of her.

"Now, how COULD we ever keep step?" she said, pausing in front of him and looking up into his face.

"I'm afraid you're right, Patty," and Kenneth looked at her with serious eyes. "But I WANT you so!" and he held out his arms.

"Nay, nay, Pauline," and Patty danced away again. "Who gets me, I think, will have to swoop down in an aeroplane, and grabble me all up and fly away with me!"

"Where do they keep aeroplanes for sale?" inquired Kenneth, looking at her meditatively.

"You dear old Ken!" and Patty danced up to him again and laid her hand on his arm. "Isn't that just exactly like you! You'd go right off and buy an airship, I believe, and try to come swooping after me!"

"Indeed I would, if it were practicable and possible."

"Yes, that's your motto: practical and possible. But you see, Mr. Ken, I like the impractical and the impossible."

"Supposing, then, that I take up those things as a serious study?"

"Oh, yes, a SERIOUS study! Is everything serious with you?"

"My love for you is very serious, Patty."

But Patty was not willing to treat it so. "That's the trouble," she said; "now if your love for me were frivolous - "

"Then it wouldn't be worth having, Patty."

"Oh, I - don't - know! At any rate, Ken, can't you mix it? Say three parts seriousness to one part frivolousness? Though I'd rather have the proportions reversed."

"Patty, you're incorrigible!"

"Good gracious! what's that? It must be something awfully nice, if I'm it."

"Well, you are it, - and I don't know what to do with you."

"You mean, you don't know what to do without me!"

"Same thing. But you'll promise me this, won't you? To think it over seriously and not decide at once."

"Yes, I'll promise that. How long do you want me to think it over, Ken?"

"The rest of your life, Patty."

"Ken, if you say such clever things as that, I'm afraid I'll fall in love with you!"

"Patty, darling, - don't tease me like that! If I thought you meant it -"

"But, anyway, Ken, if I take the rest of my life to think this thing over, I can't give you an answer till my dying day! And that seems late -"

"Patty, stop talking like that! You'll drive me crazy! Now listen, little girl, I'm going now. And you're going to think over what I've said to you. And - try to think kindly, - won't you?"

"I've never thought of you any way but kindly, Ken."

"Well, think more than kindly, then, - think lovingly. Good-night, Patty."

Kenneth held out his hand and Patty put her little hand slowly into it.

As she felt his strong, warm clasp, a mischievous impulse moved her to say, demurely: "I think it would be polite, Ken, if you kissed my hand, instead of squeezing it to pieces!"

Kenneth gave her one look, dropped a light kiss on the back of her little hand, and with a courteous bow left the room.

For a moment Patty stood where he had left her, then, as she heard the front door close, she looked curiously at the back of her hand, almost as if expecting to see a mark there.

"Dear old Ken," she said, softly, to herself, and then she went upstairs.

CHAPTER XV

AN INVITATION

Notwithstanding the experience of the evening, Patty slept dreamlessly all night, and was only awakened, when Jane came in the morning with her breakfast tray.

"Hello, Jane," she said, sleepily, opening her eyes, "will you ask Mrs. Fairfield to come up here right away?"

"What is it, Patty?" said Nan, appearing a moment later; "are you ill? Jane said you wanted me right away."

"No, I'm not ill," and Patty gave her stepmother a quizzical glance. "Sit down, Nan, and brace yourself for a shock. In me you behold a charming young debutante who has received her first proposal from a most worthy young man."

"Good gracious, Patty! Kenneth?"

"None other!" And Patty waved her hand dramatically.

"Naturally, I'm not overcome with amazement, as he spoke to Fred about it first. Kenneth always has good manners. Well, and what did you say, Patty?"

Patty eyed Nan, provokingly. "What do you think, Nancy?"

"Honestly, Patty, I haven't the slightest idea. Ken is splendid, I think, - but -"

"But what, Nan?" And Patty looked deeply interested.

"First, what did you say?"

"I won't tell you, until you tell me what you meant by 'but.'"

"Why, I only meant that Kenneth is, - well he's a dear and all that, but he's so -"

"Oh, fiddlesticks, Nan, say it out! Dull, prosaic, old-fogy, poky, slow."

"Patty, Patty! those words are too strong! Ken isn't all those things! He's only, - just a little bit -"

"Just a day and a half behind the times. Or else I'm a day and a half ahead of them. Well, Nan, that's what I told him."

"What! that he was dull and old-fogy?"

"Not exactly those terms; but in a few well-chosen words I gave him that impression, or tried to. By the way, Nan, I danced all round the room while he was proposing. Was that correct?"

"Patty, stop your nonsense! Will you never be

grown-up? You shall not make fun of Kenneth."

"Oh, Nan, I only wish I could! You might as well try to make fun of the Public Library. Kenneth is an institution. I always feel like saying to him, 'Sail on, sail on, oh, Ship of State!' or something like that. Now, wait a minute, Nan; don't you think I don't appreciate his sterling qualities. Like a Ship of State, he's made of pure granite, - oh, NO, they don't make ships of granite, do they? - I mean like the Public Library, you know. And he has solid foundations, - mental, moral, and physical. But he hasn't any fancy work about him. Even the Public Library has flags flying, - but Ken never thinks of anything as gay as a flag."

"Patty, you're talking a lot, but I do believe you know what you're saying; - it's true, dear. And are you going to marry him?"

"Marry him!" And Patty looked distinctly aggrieved. "Why, Nan, do you think for a moment I'd accept my first proposal? No, sir-ee! After I've had half a dozen, I may take one seriously, but not before. How can I tell until I've seen various sorts? Why, Nan, Kenneth didn't go down on his knees at all! I thought they always did. Didn't father, when he asked you?"

"Oh, Patty, I thought you were up-to-date! Kneeling proposals went out with the Colonials! It's only a tradition, now."

"Gracious, Nan, how experienced you are! But I don't think I shall accept anybody until he kneels to me. But don't tell anybody that, for I don't want them all doing it on purpose."

"Patty," and Nan spoke seriously, "it's all very well for you to rattle on like this, but you mustn't treat Ken's proposal lightly. He's a splendid man and he's terribly in love with you -"

"Wait a minute, Nan," and Patty was quite as earnest as the other. "Ken isn't TERRIBLY in love with me. I'd like it better if he were. He's deeply in love, even earnestly, - almost solemnly, but -"

"That's the best sort, Patty. Remember, dear, flirtation is all very well; but in the man you marry you want those qualities you've just mentioned."

"Oh, Nan, don't you be serious, too! Ken's seriousness almost finished me. And I suppose father will take the same tack! Oh, I don't want to be grown-up, - I think it's HORRID!"

Nan looked sympathetically at Patty.

"I suppose, right here," Patty went on, "I ought to burst into tears. Don't girls always cry over their first proposal? But, Nan, I feel more like giggling. I can't help it. It seems so ridiculous for Kenneth and me to go through that scene we had last evening. We've been friends so long, and then for him, all of a sudden -"

"It wasn't sudden with him, Patty. He's been in love with you for years."

"Yes, so he says. Well, Nan, I don't HAVE to marry him, do I?"

"No, of course not."

"Well, then, I'm not going to! And I don't want to be treated as if I were an ingrate because I don't! Ken is a splendid man, noble souled and all that, but I don't love him and never shall. Now please, Nan, be nice to me."

"Why, Patty, dear, I never dreamed of NOT being nice to you! I do want you to realise what you're throwing away, but if you couldn't be happy with Ken, of course, you mustn't marry him. He's a very different temperament from you, and I think myself he would be a sort of a weight on your buoyant nature. And if you're sure of your own heart, that's all there is about it. But you must tell Ken so, just as kindly as possible, for I know it will be an awful blow to the poor fellow. Did you tell him?"

"Yes, I did, but he insisted that I should think it over."

"Well, think it over. It won't hurt you to do that. And if you keep getting more and more certain that you don't love Kenneth and never will, then you'll know you're right in your decision. You're a dear girl, Patty, and I want you to marry some time, and just the right man."

"As you did."

"Yes, as I did," and Nan gave a happy smile. "You will probably marry some one nearer your own age, Patty, but you can never be any happier than Fred and I are."

"I believe you, you dear old thing! Oh, here's the mail, and I have not touched my breakfast yet."

Jane came in with a lot of letters, and Patty pounced upon one in particular.

"Here's a letter from Adele," she cried. "I hope she's coming to the city, she's been talking of it."

But instead of that news, the letter contained an invitation for Patty to come up to Fern Falls for a visit.

"Come to spend May-day," Adele wrote. "I'm having a small house party; in part, a reunion of our Christmas crowd. Daisy is here and Hal, of course, and we all want you. Invite one or two of your beaux, if you like, but don't bring any more girls; for we have two or three new neighbours with a superfluity of daughters. Come as soon as you can, and stay as long as you will, and bring your prettiest frocks. Oceans of love from me and Jim. Adele."

"That's good," said Nan, as she read the letter. "Why don't you start right off, Patty? Adele says to invite some young men if you like. You might ask Kenneth!"

"No, thank you. I don't want any of the boys. I'll be glad to get away from them for awhile. I must have some new frocks, Nan. Something Springy, you know."

"Yes, we'll go and order them to-day. I'd love to." Nan spoke absentmindedly, for she was reading her own letters, and Patty proceeded to open the rest of her mail.

That evening Kenneth came for his answer.

Patty had talked it over with her father, and had concluded the kindest thing was to tell Kenneth frankly, no.

The scene was not as difficult as Patty had feared, for Kenneth took the cheerful attitude of believing that she would yet relent.

"So long as there is no one else, Patty, girl," he said, very gently, "I'm going to hope that you will yet learn to love me. I shall never despair, until you tell me yourself that you have given your heart to some one else."

"And we'll be good friends, Ken?"

"You bet we will! You needn't think I'm down and out because you've said no, once! I'm not awfully swift, Patty, but I'm terribly persistent, - and I'm just going to keep on loving you, in hope that some day you'll come to me because you want to."

"But there's no promise, Ken."

"No, dear, no promise. Only a hope in my heart, too deep to be rooted out, that some day -"

"So - me day! So - ome day!" chanted Patty in a trilling voice, and Ken smiled in his old, friendly fashion.

"He is awfully nice," Patty said to Nan, afterward, "when he isn't proposing. There's something about Ken you can't help liking."

And Nan smiled and said, "That's so."

The days flew along, the spring frocks materialised and the grass and flowers began to be beautiful up at Fern Falls.

Patty went up there a few days before the first of May, and was welcomed by the Kenerleys with vigorous and jubilant greetings.

"You dear!" exclaimed Adele, as after a rapturous hug she held Patty off to look at her. "I do believe you're prettier than ever!"

"It's the happiness of coming up here," said Patty, smiling. "I'm so glad to come, Adele. The country in spring, - and all that, you know."

"Yes," said Adele, laughing. "You know what the Boston girl said: 'Oh, I just LOVE nature! It ADDS so!' You're like that, aren't you, Patty?"

"Exactly! but spring is all over the city, too. They're selling flowers on every street corner, and all the pedestrians wear big bunches of violets or daffodils or magnolias or something. Daisy, you're looking fine! How long have you been here?"

"I came last week," said Daisy Dow, "and I'm awfully glad to see you again, Patty."

And then Patty was whisked off to her room, and not until tea-time did she see the rest of the house party.

Then her host, Jim Kenerley, appeared, and Hal Ferris, Adele's brother, and, greatly to Patty's surprise, Philip Van Reypen.

"I didn't expect to see you here, Phil," said Patty, after she had greeted the men of the house.

"I'm only here for a short time," returned Philip; "Mrs.

Kenerley invited me to stay as long as I behaved myself; but you know, Patty, I can't do that very long."

"No, indeed! You'll be starting to-morrow morning at that rate!"

"Now, Patty, that's unkind of you. However, under your angelic influence, I may behave well enough to stay till the afternoon train."

"You're a beautiful behaver, Mr. Van Reypen," declared his hostess, "and I shan't let naughty Patty cast aspersions."

"What are those things, Adele?" asked Patty; "I'm sure I never cast anything like that at anybody, and I wouldn't hit him if I did. I can't hit the side of a barn."

"I know they say that about women," said Hal Ferris; "but I believe it's a base libel. At least, I think they could be taught to accomplish such a feat. I believe I'll organise a class of young ladies and teach them how to hit the side of a barn."

"But why hit it at all?" asked Daisy; "what has the poor barn done to be hit?"

"Lots of people get hit when they don't deserve it," said Kenerley. "But don't use our barn, Hal, use the neighbour's. Because under your tuition, your pupils might get proficient enough to hit it."

"I'm so glad to be here when it isn't winter," said Patty, looking around her. They were having tea on one of the wide verandas, which, though still enclosed with glass, had many panes open to the spring air.

"From now on, it's lovely here," said Adele; "almost every day we have one more sash open and then pretty soon we take them all out."

"It was lovely last winter, when we had tea by the hall fireplace, but this is better still," and Patty leaned back in her Japanese wicker easy-chair and nibbled contentedly at her plate of little cakes.

The tea hour at the Kenerleys' was always a pleasant affair, and in warm weather neighbours from the nearby country houses were apt to stroll over. On this occasion two or three came and Patty became acquainted with several young ladies.

"You know what I told you," said Adele to Patty, after they had left. "We have plenty of girls around here, but not many men. So for the May-party, I want you to ask a few of your friends to come up."

"All right, I will; the boys will all be glad to come. Which ones do you want?"

"I've already asked Roger Farrington, and we'll see about the others later."

"All right," said Patty, carelessly; "I've one or two new friends whom I'm sure you will like."

The next day Patty had a brilliant idea for a joke on Kit Cameron. It popped into her head quite suddenly, and she gleefully told her scheme to Adele and Daisy, as they sat together in Adele's own pleasant sitting-room.

"Doesn't Mr. Cameron know you're up here?" asked Adele.

"No; I haven't seen him for a week or two. He went South with the Homers and only came home the day I left."

The plan was carefully thought out, amid giggling and laughter, and the final result was achieved by Patty in the form of a much scribbled letter.

"Now I'm going down to copy this on Jim's typewriter," she said. And she flew downstairs to the library, from which opened a small office fitted up for Mr. Kenerley's home use.

Jim Kenerley had gone to business, and Van Reypen and Hal Ferris were playing golf, so Patty had the place to herself; and by dint of slow but persevering pounding on the typewriter, she picked out the following missive:

"Mr. Christopher Cameron: DEAR MR. CAMERON,

A few weeks ago I heard you play the violin at a concert! Oh, if I could tell you the raptures that thrilled my soul at the floods of melody you drew from the insensate strings! Only a poet's spirit, only a high-strung heart could accomplish such strains! I, too, am of a musical spirit; I, too, thrill to the notes of the great masters, if interpreted as they are by you! May I hope that you will not spurn this outburst of a sympathetic nature, and accept this tribute to your genius? Could I look for a line, - just a word, - in response to this, saying that you are glad of my appreciation? Never before have I written to a stranger. That is why I dare not use my own penmanship. Please do not seek to find out who I am, but send just a line that I may know you do not scorn my praise. Address Miss Belle Harcourt,

Carolyn Wells

Maple Bank, Conn."

The conspirators had decided upon the Maple Bank Post-office as being safer than Fern Falls, if Kit should by any chance hear that Patty had gone to the Kenerleys'.

"You know," said Patty, as she sealed the letter, "it might be mean to play this trick on anybody else, but Kit plays so many jokes on other people, he deserves it. And while he's not over-conceited, yet he's just vain enough to be tickled to death with this appreciation of his music. 'Miss Harcourt' will get an answer, all right! Come on, girls, let's get ready to go to Maple Bank."

And in a short time the three plotters were motoring over to the adjoining village to post the precious document.

Of course, they did not tell the men about this, and the three kept it an inviolate secret.

"We can hardly expect an answer for two days," said Patty, "but if I know Mr. Kit, he'll reply about as quickly as possible."

And sure enough, when the next day but one the three again invaded the little Maple Bank post-office, there was a letter from New York City for Miss Belle Harcourt.

"Read it, read it!" cried Daisy as they started homeward with their prize.

The three sat side by side in the motor, with Patty in the middle , and they all giggled , as Patty read the letter aloud.

"DEAR MISS HARCOURT:

I cannot tell you what pleasure your letter gave me. It is so delightful to learn that a stranger is interested in my poor attempts at making music. And - may I say it? - the personal charm of your letter has thrilled my heart! Only a pure, sweet, young nature could write as you do. May I not see you? Or at least will you not send me your photograph? I know I have no right to ask this, but I would so love to meet one so sympathetic and appreciative of the great art which is the ideal of my life.

With many, many thanks for your welcome letter, I am,

Very sincerely yours, CHRISTOPHER CAMERON."

"I knew he'd do it!" cried Patty. "I knew he'd fall for that flattery! Kit's a perfect dear, but he IS vain of his music, and I don't blame him. He's a wonderful violinist."

"What are you going to do next, Patty?" asked Adele. "Answer that letter?"

"Sure!" returned Patty; "but I'm not running this thing alone. We must all help make up the letter. And, Adele, haven't you some photograph that will be just right to send?"

As soon as they reached home they hunted over Adele's collection of photographs, and finally found one that Patty declared just right.

It was a picture of one of Adele's cousins, a girl of about sixteen, whose sweet young face wore an expression so soulful and languishing that it was almost comical.

"Hester hates that picture," said Adele; "she never looks that way really, - like a sick calf, - but somehow the photographer managed to catch that expression."

"She wouldn't mind if she knew, would she?" said Patty.

"Oh, mercy, no! She'd think it the best joke in the world. She lives in California, so there's little chance of Mr. Cameron ever seeing her. Now let's write the letter."

After much agony of composition and much gay fooling, the plotters produced this:

"DEAR MR. CHRISTOPHER:

I must modify your more formal name a little, - for it seems now as if I almost knew you. I tremble with fear lest some one should discover that I write to you. But I cannot help writing. I am impelled by a feeling in my soul. I send my picture and I wish it were more beautiful. For I know you love only what is good and beautiful. We must not meet, that would be TOO dangerous. But will you not write me one more precious letter that I may keep it forever?

BELLE."

There had been much discussion over the signature. Adele preferred "Yours devotedly"; Daisy wanted

"Yours adoringly"; but Patty stood out for the name alone, saying that it meant more that way.

And so the letter enclosing the picture was despatched to Kit, who received it duly.

CHAPTER XVI

BELLE HARCOURT

As quickly as possible the answer came back.

It was a rainy day, and Adele sent the chauffeur to Maple Bank after it.

The three gathered in Patty's room to hear it read, and were not surprised that it ran after this manner:

"BELLE:

How could you know the dearest way to sign yourself? Any other word would have spoiled it! But Belle! My beautiful one! I MUST see you! The picture is just what I anticipated, only more sweet and soulful. You are an angel, and I must see you or die. Do not make me wait. May I fly to Maple Bank at once? Meet me somewhere. No one will know it, - but I must look once into those dear eyes!

Your own

CHRISTOPHER."

"Oh, Kit, Kit!" exclaimed Patty, wiping tears of laughter from her eyes; "I didn't know you COULD be such an idiot! Adele, we must have him come up here."

"Oh, of course. How shall we arrange a meeting?"

"I'll tell you," said Daisy, "write him that Belle will meet him in front of the Maple Bank post-office. Then let Patty meet him, you know, and we'll sit in the car and see the fun."

"All right," Patty agreed. "WON'T he be mad when he sees ME!"

So they wrote:

"MY CHRISTOPHER:

I knew we were made for each other. I, too, feel that I must see you. But our meeting must be secret. I cannot risk my people knowing about it. So, will you meet me in front of the Maple Bank post-office at four o'clock on Thursday afternoon? I would like a more secluded place, but I dare not. The post-office is on a beautiful maple-shaded street and we can meet casually, as if we were ordinary passersby. You must only speak with me a few moments, and let me look once deep in your eyes, and then you must pass on, - out of my life forever! But I shall have at least one moment of blissful rapture! You will know me, because I shall wear white, with pink roses in my hat, and a pink parasol. I can hardly wait for Thursday! Come soon to

Your

BELLE."

"I rather guess that'll fetch him, " observed Patty,

complacently, as she sealed the envelope. "I knew Kit was a romantic goose, but I didn't suppose he'd be up to these tricks."

"Of course we'll bring him home with us, Patty," said Adele.

"Yes, he'll come fast enough."

"If he isn't too mad at you," put in Daisy.

"Oh, he won't be mad," returned Patty; "he'll be terribly cut up at first, to think I tricked him so, but he'll get over it. And I warn you, Adele, if he comes here he'll play some fearful joke on us to get even."

"I don't mind," said Adele, "I like a joke once in awhile as well as anybody else. Now if he comes Thursday, Patty, will he stay over Saturday? That's May-day, you know, and I'd like to have him here for the celebration."

"He'll be here if you ask him; even if he has to go back to the city Friday and come up again for Saturday. Phil and Roger come Saturday, you know."

Van Reypen had gone back to town for a few days, and Hal Ferris was also away on business, which was one reason why the girls had plunged so interestedly into their merry scheme.

Thursday afternoon they started for Maple Bank in time to be at the post-office before four o'clock, and witness the arrival of Mr. Cameron.

Patty looked her dainty best, in a white linen, with a

broad-brimmed hat wreathed with pink roses. Her pink parasol was flounced with chiffon and adorned with a bunch of pink roses, and two rose blooms were tucked in her belt.

"Rather summery garb, for the last of April," said Patty, gazing at herself in Adele's long mirror; "but I said I'd wear white before I thought. However, it's a lovely day, and with my motor coat I'll be warm enough going over."

They started off in high spirits, and reached the post-office at quarter before four. Kit was already there, walking calmly up and down the maple-shaded village street, and apparently waiting with properly concealed impatience.

In accordance with directions, the chauffeur drove right past the post-office and around a corner, where the three conspirators might indulge in a burst of laughter.

"I shan't appear until a few minutes after four," said Patty; "it isn't feminine to keep an appointment on time."

So they went up and down some other streets until just the right time, and then Patty got out of the car, as she intended to walk to the tryst.

The car, with Adele and Daisy, whizzed away and took up a position exactly opposite the post-office, stopping there to watch the show.

Of course Cameron paid no attention to this car, and continued to patrol the sidewalk with slow, even steps.

At last, as he walked along, he saw a girl in white coming toward him. Her pink parasol completely concealed her face, but Cameron knew it was his "Belle."

He walked on slowly, and Patty did too, until they met and both stopped. Gently he raised the intruding parasol and turned it to one side.

But even then, he could not see Patty's face, for she had arranged her broad-brimmed hat to droop over it, and she hung her head as if in extreme shyness. But she put out her hand and Cameron clasped it in his own.

"Belle," he murmured, "MY Belle! Look at me, please!"

Suddenly Patty lifted her head, and smiled into Kit Cameron's face.

He took a step backward, and staggered almost as if he would fall.

"Patty Fairfield!" he exclaimed, "what does this mean? Why are you here? I expected - oh, I beg your pardon - I - I'm aw-awfully glad to see you."

Adele and Daisy, watching them, were convulsed at Cameron's baffled surprise. They could almost hear what he said. They could see how he tried to pull himself together, and they could see Patty speechless with laughter, as she enjoyed the joke on Kit.

"What are YOU doing in Maple Bank?" she said, as soon as she could speak for laughing.

Kit looked at her gravely. "I came expressly to meet a girl in a white frock and pink roses. I don't see any other around, so - it might as well be you!"

"You needn't try to turn it off so carelessly," said Patty. "Own up that you're caught! What was your girl's name?"

"Belle - My Belle - " And Cameron rolled his eyes in such soulful manner, that Patty went off in another paroxysm.

"Oh, you Joke King, you! Nobody can trick you, can they? Do you own up?"

"Own up what? that I'd rather see you than any other belle? Certainly, I'll own that. But my time is up. You know we were only to gaze once into each other's eyes and then part forever!" And Kit gazed into her eyes as if it were indeed the last time.

"That'll do," said Patty, laughing again. "The farce is over. Now come and be real. Your own beautiful real self. Come and meet my friends."

"Who?" said Kit, as he accompanied Patty across the street.

"Here he is," sang out Patty, as they reached the car. "Mrs. Kenerley, - Miss Dow, - may I present Mr. Cameron, the celebrated violin virtuoso."

Adele greeted him warmly, and Daisy smiled on him, and Cameron's own delightful manner soon made them all friends.

"Jump in and go home with us, Mr. Cameron," said Adele, turning down a side seat in the car.

"But my stay in Maple Bank is limited," said Kit. "I'm due to take the next train back to New York."

"Come back with us to tea, anyway," said Adele.

"You can stay to dinner, too," said Patty, "and take a late train down from Fern Falls."

"But you see, though I dressed with particular care to meet a very charming young lady, I didn't expect to dine with her."

"Oh, no matter," said Adele; "we won't be formal to-night. But if you will, Mr. Cameron, we'd like to have you come back on Saturday for our May-day celebration."

"Will I!" said Kit; "you're awfully good to ask me, Mrs. Kenerley, after you've discovered what a wicked young man I am, thus to follow up invitations from strange ladies. But you see the photograph that came to me was so charming that the temptation was irresistible."

"If you'd known it was only me, you wouldn't have come, would you?" asked Patty.

Kit regarded her solemnly. Then he waved his hand, as if dismissing a question of no moment. "It doesn't matter," he said, "all young ladies in pink and white look alike to me."

"Then I'm glad I'm not in pink and white," said Daisy,

who was looking very pretty in a blue linen frock, with wide black ribbons.

"So am I," and Kit smiled at her approvingly. "You look so different, it's a pleasure to observe you."

Cameron had a charming way of talking nonsense, and before they reached home both Daisy and Adele had taken a decided liking to the gay young man.

They had tea on the glass-paned veranda, and it was not until they were all comfortably seated, with their teacups in hand, that Cameron said, casually: "Oh, by the way, Patty, I have a note for you from Mrs. Fairfield, and a parcel."

He took from his pocket a letter and a little box.

"Oh, thank you," said Patty, taking them "May I?" she added, as she opened the note.

As Patty read, her face grew longer and her eyes grew bigger. As she finished, she looked at Cameron, who was gazing at her with his eyes full of laughter.

"You Kit!" she exclaimed; "oh, you Kit Cameron! Can nobody EVER get ahead of you? Girls, listen to this! It's a note from Nan, and she says: 'Dear Patty: Mr. Cameron says he's going to see you to-morrow. Has Adele invited him to Fern Falls? How nice for you all. He won't tell me how she happened to do so, but I suppose it was through you. I'm sending you by him your pearl pin, which you forgot. Oceans of love, from Nan.' Now, how in the name of common sense, did you happen to tell Nan that you were coming to see me?"

"Why, I was there last night, and I knew I was coming up here to-day; so I told her, and she asked me to bring your pin. And I said I would. That's all."

"But how did you know you were coming here?" persisted Patty.

"I didn't know I was coming here, and I didn't tell Mrs. Fairfield I was. I only told her I should see you. I can't help what she assumed, - and I have delivered the pin in safety."

"But how did you know you were going to see me?"

"My dear child, do you suppose for one minute that I fell for that Belle Harcourt business? Didn't you know that I would know that that very first letter was written by your fairy fingers?"

"Why, Mr. Cameron!" exclaimed Adele, "weren't you really fooled?"

"You WERE!" exclaimed Daisy. "You were at first, anyway."

"Not for a minute, Miss Dow," and Kit smiled lazily at her. "I'm not over-modest about my wonderful musical genius, but somehow I couldn't believe that a stranger appreciated me so highly. I just COULDN'T believe it, and something told me that it wasn't quite all it sounded. Then, says I to myself, if it isn't a real Belle Harcourt it's most probably Patty Fairfield. I had no idea you were away, but I telephoned the house, and some of your menials told me you were at Fern Falls. I had never heard of Fern Falls, but it was me for the atlas, and after much study, I unearthed Fern Falls and found it to be very decidedly adjacent to Maple Bank. So I put away my atlas, got down my arithmetic, and by its artful aid I managed to put two and two together. If I had found any one else but Patty Fairfield under that pink parasol, I should have been the most surprised man under the Stars and Stripes!"

"I think you're perfectly horrid!" cried Patty; "just perfect-ly hor-rid!"

"You don't really, you know," and Kit smiled at her, calmly, "you're just as ready to admit yourself tricked, as I was."

Patty went off into a peal of laughter at the thought of how she had insisted that Kit should own up to being tricked, when they met; but she felt a little chagrined that her joke had fallen through.

"I'm glad of it," declared Adele, "for I may as well confess, Mr. Cameron, it had prejudiced me against you to think you would write those letters to a stranger."

"Oh, I wouldn't, Mrs. Kenerley," said Kit, with exaggerated earnestness. "Honest and truly, I wouldn't! I NEVER write letters to strangers, unless I'm SURE the strangers are Patty Fairfield. And I'm sure I shouldn't dare to write a letter to the young lady of the photograph that came to me. She looked like an angel in the last stages of nervous prostration."

"That's exactly what she did look like," said Adele, laughing. "I must tell Hester that! She's a school-girl cousin of mine, Mr. Cameron, and if she were here, she'd enjoy this two-story joke as well as any of us."

Cameron stayed to dinner, as he said, to make his peace with Mr. Kenerley when he came home, but really because he wanted to remain with the pleasant house party.

Hal Ferris came home at dinner time, too, and was greatly diverted by the whole story of the Belle Harcourt joke.

After dinner, it was warm enough to sit out on the veranda till time for Kit to go to the train.

At last the chauffeur brought the little runabout to the door, and Kit took leave of the merry group.

"Be sure to come back on Saturday morning," said Adele, as she shook hands with him.

"Trust me for that, Mrs. Kenerley. I'm so delighted with the invitation, I'm afraid I'll get here too soon."

"Come up on the noon train. The May party's at four o'clock. And now you must fly or you'll lose your train."

"Parting is SUCH sweet sorrow," said Kit, as he took Patty's hand, to say good-bye to her last.

Patty followed him down the steps of the veranda, and he was about to step into the car, when he said, "Come on down to the station with me."

"I will," said Patty, impulsively, and as there was no time to discuss the matter, she sprang into the car. Kit jumped in after her, and slammed the door and they were off.

"We've eloped," Cameron called back, as they whizzed away.

"All right," Adele called after them; "send Patty back by the chauffeur. There are extra wraps under the seat."

"What a duck you are to come!" said Kit, as they swung out through the gate.

"I didn't mean to; but I jumped in before I thought."

"Always jump in before you think, - that is, if I'm around. If there's any danger of drowning, I'll pull you out."

"Oh, I can swim. Kit, I don't see how you knew I wrote that letter."

"Patty, it was plain as day on the face of it. Why, it sounded just like you from start to finish. Of course, if you had been in New York, I should have tried to suspect somebody else, but when I found you were staying only about six miles from Maple Bank, I knew it was you."

"Never mind, some day I'll play a joke on you."

"Thought you didn't approve of them."

"I don't, for other people. But you're so fond of them I feel as if I ought to do all I can for you."

"All right, joke away, little girl. I don't mind. I say, Poppycheek, what's this May-day business? An old-fashioned picnic?"

"Not exactly. It's a new-fashioned picnic. But they crown a May-queen, and all that sort of foolishness."
"And who is to be queen?"

"Belle Harcourt."

"MY Belle! Oh, I'm glad of that. And so Princess Poppycheek is going to be made a queen! Well, so long as you're my Belle, you may be anybody's queen you like."

"I like an awful lot of people."

"Mostly men."

"No, sir! The men mostly like me. I like mostly girls. Don't you think Daisy Dow's charming and pretty?"

"Yes, she is a very pretty girl. You're fond of her?"

"I am now. I didn't like her at first, but I think it was because I didn't understand her. But now we're awfully good chums."

"And so you don't like the men?"

"Nonsense! Of course I do. I adore them. But not as much as I do my girl friends. And sometimes I think I like my married friends best of all. Aren't the Kenerleys just dear?"

"Then you'd like me better if I were married?"

"Yes, indeed. Will you get married, to please me?"

"Oh, anything to oblige. Will you pick out the lady?"

"Why, yes, if you want me to. There's Daisy Dow."

"Yes, there's Daisy Dow. But here's Patty Fairfield. I'd ever so much rather marry her! How about it, Poppycheek?"

"Nonsense, Kit, don't be silly."

"It isn't silly. You said you wanted me to be married and I'm awfully anxious to please you."

"Oh, do you want to marry me just to please me?"

"Well, I'm interested in the scheme on my own account, too."

"Well, don't bother me about it, now. I hate to answer questions in a speeding motor-car."

"Shall I tell him to slow down?" And Kit leaned forward toward the chauffeur.

"Mercy, no! you'll hardly catch your train now. A little faster, Jacques."

"Yes, Miss," and the chauffeur threw on a little more speed.

"Poppycheek, you rascal, I intended to miss that train."

"Well, you don't do it! see? We've enough to do to-morrow, without you bothering around. You can come up Saturday, but to-morrow we're going to be awfully busy."

"Van Reypen coming?"

Carolyn Wells

"Of course. A party isn't a party without Phil."

"Huh! I'm not afraid of him. I can cut Van Reypen out any day in the week!"

"Not Saturdays. That's his great day." And Patty laughed tantalisingly.

"Just you wait and see! I'm not afraid! Bye-bye, Poppycheek."

They had reached the station just as the train was drawing out. Kit sprang from the car, slammed the door after him, and striding across the platform, swung on to the moving steps. He waved his hand at Patty and was gone.

"Home, Jacques," she said.

CHAPTER XVII

MAY-DAY

May-Day, contrary to its custom, was a perfectly beautiful, balmy, sunshiny day.

Adele drew a long sigh of relief when she opened her eyes to this fact, for as the hostess of a large and elaborate garden party she had no care so great as the question of weather. And as all outdoors was a mass of warm sunshine, she felt sure of the success of her fete.

After luncheon she ordained that Patty should go to her room for a nap, as she had worked hard all the morning, and must not look fagged at her coronation.

"Make Daisy go too, then," said Patty, pouting, as she started upstairs.

"No, Daisy can do as she likes. She isn't tired and you are."

"But then Daisy will be here when the boys come, and I won't."

"You insatiable little coquette! You go right straight to your room and go to bed! You hear me?"

240   Carolyn Wells

"Yes, ma'am, but I can't sleep. I'm too 'cited!"

"Well, you can rest. Get yourself into a kimono, - and I'll come up in a minute and tuck you up."

Adele went up in a few moments and found Patty leaning far out of her window.

"What ARE you doing, child? Don't lean out so far; you'll fall!"

Patty proceeded to draw herself back into the room. "Of course I won't fall, Adele! I was only trying to breathe all this whole May-day into my lungs at once. It's so beautiful."

"It is, I know; but, Patty, darling, you MUST behave yourself. Lie down and take a little sleepy-by till three o'clock. Then you can get dressed for the party."

"'I will be good, dear mother, I heard a sweet child say,'" trilled Patty, as she took down her hair and put on a kimono.

Then Adele tucked her up on the couch, in a nest of pillows and under a soft down quilt.

"Of course I trust you," she said, as she patted her shoulder, "oh, OF COURSE I trust you! but all the same, my lady, I'm going to lock you in!"

"What!" cried Patty.

But even as she spoke, Adele had scurried across the room, drawn out the key, and was already locking the door from the other side.

"Well!" thought Patty, "that's a high-handed performance! I don't really care, though. Now that I'm here, so comfy, I realise that I am tired." And in about two minutes Patty was sound asleep.

It was nearly an hour before she opened her eyes, and then with a little yawn she lazily wondered if it were time to get up. She glanced at the clock on her dressing-table, and as it was only half-past two, she felt sure that Adele would not come to her release until three o'clock. She lay there, her eyes wandering idly about the room, when she saw a startling sight. The floor, near her couch, was fairly strewn with sprays of apple blossoms. At first she thought she must be dreaming, and rubbed her eyes to be sure she was awake. Putting her hand down outside the silken coverlet, she touched a spray of blossoms, and picking it up looked at it wonderingly. There could be no doubt. They were real apple blossoms, and they were really there! What could it mean?

"Of course," she said to herself, "either Adele or Daisy came in while I was asleep and brought me these flowers, and sprinkled them on the floor for fun. It must have been Daisy, for Adele is too busy. How much nicer Daisy is than she used to be. And maybe that's not fair. Probably she always was just as nice, only I wasn't nice to her. Or I didn't know how to take her. Oh, my gracious!"

The last words were spoken aloud, and in a very surprised voice, the reason for which was, that a lot of apple blossoms had come flying through the open window and landed on the floor beside her. "It must be Daisy," she thought, "Adele won't let her in here, and she's trying to get my attention this way!"

Patty scrambled off the couch, her long golden hair a tangled mass around her shoulders, and her blue silk negligee edged with swansdown draped about her.

She went to the window, which was a long French one, opening like doors onto a tiny balcony. She stepped out on the balcony and looked down.

And then, in her surprise, she almost fell over the railing, for down below on the lawn, with his smiling face looking up into hers, stood, - Bill Farnsworth.

Patty gave a squeal of delight. "BILL!" she cried, "Little Billee"

"Look out, Apple Blossom!" he called back, in his big, cheery voice, "don't fall out of that balcony, and break your blessed neck! But if you want to jump, I'll catch you," and he held out his arms.

"No! I don't want to jump! Oh, Little Billee, I didn't know you were coming! Did you throw in the apple blossoms?"

"No, no, oh, NO! A passing highwayman threw those in! Why, what made you think *I*'d do such a thing?"

"Only because you still have a few left in your pockets," said Patty, laughing, for, sure enough, Bill had ends of blossom sprays sticking out of all his pockets.

"You see I didn't know how many it would take to wake you up," he said.

"How did you know I was up here?"

"Daisy told me. Adele wouldn't tell me, - said you must sleep, or some such foolishness. Get into your togs and come down, won't you?"

For the first time Patty realised that her hair was hanging about her shoulders and her costume was, to say the least, informal, and with another little squeal, she sprang back into her room and closed the window doors.

Then she went and looked at herself in the mirror.

"Well, you don't look an absolute fright," she said, to the smiling reflection she saw there. "But to think of Bill being here! Little Billee! Bless his old heart!"

And then Patty flew at her toilet. Everything had been laid in readiness, and she began to draw on her white silk stockings and dainty slippers.

She was sitting before her mirror, doing her hair, when the key turned and Adele came in.

"For goodness' sake, Patty Fairfield! WHERE did all these flowers come from?"

"They came in at the window, ma'am, before I closed it," said Patty, demurely.

"Came in at the window! Nonsense, how could they do that?"

"Oh, the breeze was awful strong, and it just blew them in."

"Silly child ! But I say, Patty, hurry up and

get dressed!"

"I AM hurrying!" and Patty provokingly twisted up her curls with slow, deliberate motions.

"You're NOT! you're dawdling horribly! But you wouldn't, if you knew who was downstairs!"

"Who?"

"Oh, you're very indifferent, aren't you? Well, you wouldn't be so indifferent if you knew who's downstairs."

"Not, by any chance, Bill Farnsworth?"

"Yes! that's just exactly who it is! How did you ever guess? Are you glad?"

"Yes, of course I am," and Patty's pink cheeks dimpled as she smiled frankly at Adele. "I'm just crazy to see Bill again!"

"Look here, Patty," and Adele spoke somewhat seriously, "I want to say something to you, - and yet I hate to. But I feel as if I ought to."

"My stars! Adele, what IS the dreadful thing?"

Patty paused in her hairdressing and, with brush in one hand and mirror in the other, she stared at Adele.

"Why, you see, Patty, I know you do like Bill, and - I don't want you to like him too much."

"What DO you mean?"

"Oh, nothing. It even sounds silly to say it to you, as a warning. But, dear, I feel I MUST tell you. He's engaged."

"Oh, is he?" Patty tossed her head, and then went on arranging her hair, but the pink flush on her cheek deepened. "Are you sure?" she said, carelessly.

"Well, I'm not sure that he's engaged, really," and Adele wrinkled her pretty brow, as she looked at Patty; "but he told me last winter that all his life was bound up in Kitty, and he loved her with all his heart, or something like that."

"Kitty who?"

"I can't remember her other name, although he told me."

"How did Bill happen to tell you this, Adele?"

"He was here, and I was chaffing him about one of the Crosby girls, and then he told me that about Kitty. And somehow I thought you ought to know it."

"Oh, fiddlesticks, Adele, as if I cared! I can't understand why you should think *I* would care if Mr. Farnsworth were engaged to forty-'leven girls. It's nothing to me."

"Of course I know it isn't, Patty; but I just wanted to tell you."

"All right, honey; I'm glad you did. Now go on downstairs, and I'll be down in a few minutes."

Adele ran away and Patty proceeded to don her royal robes.

The coronation gown was of white chiffon, having no decoration save tiny bunches and garlands of flowers. It was not made in the prevailing fashion, but copied from a quaint old picture and was very becoming to its wearer.

Her golden curls were loosely massed and a few flowers adorned them.

Patty sat a moment in front of her mirror, talking to herself, as she often did.

"Of course Little Billee is engaged," she said to herself; "he's too nice a man not to be. And I hope his Kitty is a lovely, sweet, charming girl. I don't think, as an engaged man, he had any business to throw flowers in at my window, but I suppose that was because we've always been good friends. I don't see how he could tear himself away from the charming Kitty long enough to come East, but he's always flying across the continent on his business trips."

Daisy came into Patty's room then, and the two girls went downstairs together.

The guests had gathered for the garden party, and were dotted over the lawns or grouped on the veranda.

"Thank goodness it's a warm day," said Patty, as they went down the stairs. "Sometimes on May-day we have to go around in fur coats."

At the foot of the staircase Bill Farnsworth waited to

greet Patty.

He came forward with an eager smile and took her two hands in his.

"Little Apple Blossom!" he exclaimed; "Patty Pink-and-White!"

For the life of her, Patty could not be as cordial as she would have been if Adele had not told her what she did. But though she tried to speak a genuine welcome, she only succeeded in saying, "How do you do, Mr. Farnsworth?" in a cool little voice.

Big Bill looked at her in amazement.

"You gave me a better greeting than that from your window," he said, in laughing reproach. "I still have an apple blossom left. May I give it to you?" and Bill produced a small but perfect spray which he proceeded to pin on the shoulder of Patty's gown.

"My costume is complete," said Patty, with a smiling dissent; "it doesn't need any additional flower."

"It needs this one to make it perfect," said Farnsworth, calmly, and indeed the pretty blossom was no detriment to the effect.

"Oh, Phil, how gorgeous you look!" and Patty abruptly turned from Farnsworth to admire Van Reypen's get-up.

"Me, too!" exclaimed Hal Ferris, stepping up to be admired. The men's decorations consisted of garlands draped across their shoulders and tied with huge bows of ribbon. On their heads they wore classic wreaths which Daisy and Hal had made, and which were really not unbecoming. The procession formed in the hall, and went out across the lawn to the May Queen's throne.

Hal Ferris and Van Reypen headed the line, Hal being the sceptre-bearer and Philip the crown-bearer.

Daisy followed these, carrying a silk banner which waved in the breeze, and she was followed by Baby May, carrying a basket of blossoms, which she scattered as she went along.

Patty came next, and surely a fairer May queen never went to her coronation. Patty's blonde beauty was well suited to the costume and floral decorations she wore, and she looked like a vision of Spring, incarnate, as she walked smilingly along. Behind her came Kit and Roger, who were Court Jesters. Their costumes were most elaborate, of the recognised style for jesters, and they carried baubles which provoked great merriment.

As Farnsworth had not been expected, there was no part for him on the program, but he calmly declared that he would be the band. He had brought a cornet, upon which he was a really fine performer, and he took up his place at the end of the line and played gay and merry music to which they marched.

The affair was exceedingly informal, and those in the procession chatted as they passed the guests who were mere lookers-on.

Baby May, indeed, left her place to run to her mother and give her a flower , and then dutifully returned to escort Patty.

The throne was under a bower made of evergreen boughs and trailing vines, interspersed with apple blossoms and other flowers.

As the procession neared the throne, Ferris, with his long gold sceptre, struck an attitude on one side, and Van Reypen, who carried the crown on a white satin cushion, took his place on the other side.

Daisy as Maid of Honour and Baby May as Flower Girl took their stand, and the two Court Jesters danced to their appointed places.

This left Patty alone, and, as there had been no rehearsal, she was a little uncertain what to do, when Farnsworth stepped forward and took her hand and gracefully led her to the throne, where he seated her in state. Then he made a profound bow and stepped away to one side.

Van Reypen came forward, and with a gay little impromptu speech, put a floral crown on Patty's head, and Ferris presented her with the long gilded sceptre.

Patty made a little speech of humorous greeting, and the coronation was declared over, and Patty was Queen of the May.

The guests came thronging around to talk to the pretty queen, and then they all went to the tea-tent. This gay and festive place was decorated with flowers and flags, and a delightful feast was served.

" Will you have an ice, Patty?" asked Farnsworth, "or

something more substantial?"

"Here you are, Patty; I know what you want." and Kit Cameron came up with a cup of hot bouillon and a sandwich.

"Yes, indeed, Kit, I'm famishing. Thank you so much," and Patty ignored Farnsworth's remark entirely, and beamed pleasantly on Kit.

Farnsworth looked at her curiously for a moment, and then walked away.

He sat down by Daisy Dow, and said abruptly:

"What's the matter with Patty, that she doesn't like me any more?"

"Nonsense, Bill; she does like you."

"No, she doesn't. She's cool as a cucumber. She used to like me, but she's changed all through. I s'pose she likes those other fellows better - and I don't blame her."

"They're both awfully gone on her," and Daisy looked at Cameron and Van Reypen hovering around Patty, who seemed to be sharing her favours equally between them.

"I don't belong here," said Farnsworth, gloomily. "I'm out of my element. I belong out West, riding over the plains and untrammelled by conventions."

"Don't be a goose, Bill," and Daisy looked at him kindly. "You've better manners than lots of these

Eastern men, and you have a whole lot more innate kindliness."

"That's good of you, Daisy," and Bill flashed her a grateful look. "But I know the difference myself; I'm uncouth and awkward where those chaps are correct and elegant. I'm going back to Arizona and stay there."

"All because Patty Fairfield didn't welcome you with open arms!"

A flush rose to Big Bill's handsome face. "It is partly that, Daisy, but I can't blame her. There's no reason why that exquisite little piece of humanity should want to have anything to do with me, - a big bear of a man."

"Honestly, Bill, you ought not to belittle yourself like that. I'm ashamed of you. But I'll tell you one thing: Patty is sometimes a little perverse. She can't seem to help it. She's a perfect dear, but she is a coquette. If you ask me, I think the more glad she is to see you, the more likely she is to be cool to you."

"Nonsense, Daisy! what sort of talk is that! Why should she act that way?"

Bill's straightforward gaze of blank amazement made Daisy laugh, but she only said: "I can't tell you why she does such things, but she does all the same."

Just then Hal Ferris came up and monopolised Daisy's attention, and Farnsworth, imagining himself in the way, strolled off. He joined the laughing group that was gathered around Patty, but he stood moodily silent, listening while she chaffed the others.

"It's getting chilly," Patty said, at last, "and I think it's too late to stay outdoors any longer. May parties are all very well while the sun shines. But as queen, I issue a royal mandate that now we all go in the house and dance."

"And as First Goldstick-in-Waiting, I claim the first dance with the queen," and Philip Van Reypen tucked Patty's hand through his arm and led her away to the house.

"And I claim the Maid of Honour," and Kit Cameron led Daisy away.

"Hold on," cried Hal Ferris, "the Maid of Honour is my partner."

"Possession is nine points of the law," and Hal gaily retained Daisy's hand in his own, lest she should escape him.

But there were plenty of other gay and merry maidens of the court, and soon several couples were whirling up and down through the great hall.

Farnsworth stood apart, not joining in the dance, and presently Adele came up to him.

"Dance with me, Bill," she said, with the freedom of long acquaintance.

"Thank you," said Farnsworth, and in a moment they had joined the other couples. Bill was a perfect dancer, and when they stopped, Adele said: "Why don't you dance with Patty? She is a lovely dancer. I'd like to see you two dance together."

Still with a grave face, Bill crossed the room to where Patty was standing.

"Miss Fairfield," he said, politely, "our hostess has ordained that I dance this dance with you." He clicked his heels together, and made a low military bow.

"Indeed," said Patty, coolly, "but the Queen of May takes no one's orders, not even those of her beloved hostess."

"Then you refuse?" and Farnsworth looked Patty straight in the eyes.

"Of course I refuse," and she gave her little head a disdainful toss. "This dance belongs to Mr. Van Reypen."

Philip was just passing, and as Patty laid her hand on his arm, he stopped.

"Certainly it does," he said, but it was easy to be seen that the dance was as much a surprise to him as it was a pleasure.

Farnsworth looked after the two, as they danced away. And then he turned on his heel and went in search of Adele.

CHAPTER XVIII

MOONLIGHT

The May party was over, but a few of the guests, besides those staying in the house, remained for dinner.

"Shall I change my frock, Adele, or keep on this toggery for dinner?" said Patty.

"Oh, keep that on. You may as well be Queen of May as long as you can."

So Patty kept on her pretty, picturesque costume, and when dinner time came she made up her mind to ask Adele to seat her next to Farnsworth. But as the company paired off to go to dinner Big Bill was nowhere visible.

"Where's Mr. Farnsworth?" asked Patty, casually, of Jim Kenerley.

"Oh, he's gone. We expected him to stay the week-end, but he said he was due at another country house party, farther on somewhere, and he couldn't even stay for dinner."

Patty was sorry she had acted so rude to Bill, and sorry

that he had gone. "But," she said to herself, by way of extenuation, "I didn't want to dance with anybody who asked me to because his hostess commanded him! He never even said he wanted to dance with me himself, but only that Adele said he must. But I do think he was mean to go away without saying good-bye to me!"

However, it was not Patty's nature to let her mind dwell on a disappointment, and she promptly proceeded to forget all about Mr. Farnsworth, and to turn her mind to her present partner. This happened to be Kit Cameron, and as he was in his gayest mood she responded and their conversation was of the merriest sort.

After dinner, Kit persuaded Patty to walk on the veranda for a bit of exercise. There was a large swing-seat, upholstered in red, which he declared was just the place for a tete-a-tete.

"But it's too cold," objected Patty.

"I'll get you a wrap," and Kit flew into the house and procured a long cloak, in which he enveloped Patty, and they sat in the swing together.

"What became of the Colossal Cowboy?" said Kit; "I thought he was here for the weekend."

"I thought so, too," returned Patty, "but it seems he had another engagement."

"I'm glad of it. You're altogether too fond of him."

"Fond of him! What do you mean? I'm nothing of the sort. Why, I scarcely spoke to him."

"I know it. That's what gave you away."

"Don't be a silly! I haven't the slightest interest in Mr. William Farnsworth, or his comings and goings."

"You'd rather have me here, wouldn't you?"

"Oh, EVER so much rather!" And Patty spoke with such intense enthusiasm that she was very evidently joking.

"But really, Patty, let's be in earnest just for a minute. Wouldn't you rather have me around than anybody?"

"Why, I don't know; I never thought about it."

"Think about it now, then. Honest, I mean it."

"Oh, don't mean things. It's too heavenly a night to talk seriously."

"Isn't it a wonderful night? Do you know a house party like this and moonlight on a veranda, like this, always goes to my head. I think week-ending is apt to go to one's head, anyway. But let it go. Let it go to your head, too."

"I don't think I'd better," and Patty spoke hesitatingly; "I might say something foolish."

"Oh, do, Patty! DO say something foolish! If you don't, I shall."

"Well, go on, then."

" May I, Patty? May I tell you that I've simply lost my

heart to you, - you beautiful little May Queen!"

"And is that what you call foolish?" Patty pouted, adorably.

"Yes, it's foolish, because I know there's no hope for me. I know you don't care one least scrap of a speck for me! Now, do you?"

"If you're so positive yourself, why ask me?"

"Oh, I MIGHT be mistaken, you know. Oh, if I only MIGHT! Patty, DEAR little Patty, couldn't you be my princess? My own Princess Poppycheek."

"I've been your Belle," and Patty laughed merrily at the recollection.

"There you go, laughing at me! I knew you would. That shows you don't care anything for me. If you did, you wouldn't laugh at me!"

"Oh, yes, I would! the more I care for people the more I laugh at them, - always."

"You must be simply crazy over me then! If you don't stop laughing I won't swing you any more."

"Oh, yes, do, it's lovely to swing back and forth in the moonlight like this. The May party was pretty, wasn't it?"

"You're just trying to change the subject. But I won't have it changed. Let's go back to it. Patty, couldn't you stop laughing at me long enough to learn to care for me a little?"

"How can I tell? I don't know how long it would take to learn to care for you a little. And, anyway, I do care for you a little, - but only a very, very little."

"Yes, I know that. You don't fool me any. You wouldn't care if you NEVER saw me again."

"Why, Kit Cameron, I would SO! If I though I'd never see you again - I'd - I'd - I'd drown myself!"

"YES you WOULD! You little witch, how can you trifle with me like that, when my heart is just breaking for you?"

"Oh, come now, Kit, it isn't as bad as that! And let me tell you something. Do you know I think you are one of the very nicest friends I ever had, and I'm not going to have our friendship spoiled by any foolishness! So you might as well stop right where you are now. That is, if you're in earnest. If you're just talking foolishness on account of the moonlight - and all, - I don't mind. But I won't have you serious about it."

"All right, Poppycheek. I'm pretty serious, or I would be if you'd let me, but if you don't want it you shan't have it."

"Well, I don't. I don't want seriousness from anybody. And, anyway, Kit, I'd be afraid of seriousness from you."

"Why, Patty?"

"'Cause it would probably turn out to be a practical joke."

"Joke nothing! The regard I have for you, Miss Poppycheek Fairfield, is too everlasting real to have any joke about it!"

"And the friendship I have for you, Mr. Kit Cameron, is so nice and real, that I'm going to keep it up."

Patty knew from the undertones of Kit's voice that he was very much in earnest, and as she felt no interest in him beyond that of a good friend, she shrank from wounding his feelings by letting him go on further. And so she determinedly led the conversation further and further away from personal matters, and soon she gaily declared that it was getting too late for moonlight chat and she was going in the house.

Kit followed her in, and though he showed in no way the appearance of a rejected suitor, he was quieter than usual and less inclined to merriment. "He'll get over it," said Patty to herself, after she reached her room that night. "I s'pose all girls have to go through with these scenes, sooner or later. But I didn't mind Kit so much, because he was nice and sensible about it."

Then Daisy came in for a kimono confab, and perched herself on the edge of Patty's bed.

"What's the matter between you and Bill Farnsworth, Patty?" she asked without prelude of any sort.

"Nothing," said Patty, as she took the hairpins from a long shining strand of hair.

"There is, too. He asked me why you were so cool to him."

"He did! Well, I'm sure I don't know what he meant, for I wasn't cool to him, - or anything else. I treated him politely, as I would any casual friend."

"Politely! I saw you refuse to dance with him, myself. If you call THAT polite!"

"If you want to know, Daisy, that was because he didn't want to dance with me. He said he only asked me because Adele insisted upon it."

"Patty, it's none of my business, but I do think you might be nicer to Bill, for I know he thinks an awful lot of you."

"Why, Daisy Dow! why should he think a lot of me when he's as good as engaged to another girl?"

"Engaged! Bill Farnsworth engaged! nothing of the sort. I know better."

"But he is. Adele told me so. Or, if he isn't engaged, he's very much in love with a girl named Kitty. Do you know her?"

"Kitty who? Where is she?"

"I don't know, I'm sure. But he told Adele his whole heart and life were bound up in this Kitty Somebody. So I'm sure I don't see any reason why I should be running after him."

"I can't imagine you running after anybody, Patty. You don't need to, for the boys all run after you. But it's very queer I never heard of this Kitty. I've known Bill for years. Let me see; there was Kate Morton, - but I never thought Bill cared especially for her. And anyway, I can't imagine calling HER Kitty! She's as tall and straight as an Indian!"

"Well, Bill calls her Kitty; Adele said so."

"Oh, is it Kate Morton, then? Did Adele say that?"

"No, Adele said she couldn't remember the girl's last name. And I don't care if it's Kate Morton or Kathleen Mavourneen! It's nothing to me what kind of a girl Bill Farnsworth likes."

"Of course it isn't. I know you never liked Bill."

"I did SO! I DO like him, but just the same as I like all the other boys."

"Then what makes you turn pink every time Bill's name is mentioned, and never when you speak of anybody else?"

"I don't! And if I did, it wouldn't mean anything. I'm not specially interested in anybody, Daisy, but if I were, I wouldn't sit up and blush about it. You like Bill an awful lot, yourself."

"I do like him," said Daisy, frankly; "and I always have. He's a splendid man, Patty, one of the biggest, best natures I know. Why, at school we used to call him Giant Greatheart, - he was so thoroughly noble and kind to everybody."

"Well, I'm sick of hearing his praises sung, so you'll please change the subject."

Daisy was quite willing to do this, for she had no wish to annoy Patty, and the girls chatted of other matters until Adele came along and sent them both to bed.

The next day was Sunday, and Patty didn't come downstairs until time for the midday dinner.

"I think you might have come down earlier," said Van Reypen, reproachfully, as Patty came smilingly down the staircase. "I wanted you to go for a walk this morning; it's simply great out in the sunshine."

"I'll go after dinner," said Patty; "isn't it funny why people have dinner at one o'clock, just because it's Sunday?"

"I'm glad of it. It'll give us the whole afternoon for our walk."

"Good gracious! if I walk the whole afternoon you'll have to bring me home in a wheelbarrow!"

"We won't walk far enough for that. If you get tired, we'll sit on a mossy mound in a bosky dell, or some such romantic spot."

After dinner, Philip held Patty to her promise of going for a walk. She didn't care about it especially, really preferring to stay with the gay group gathered on the veranda, but Philip urged it, and Patty allowed herself to be persuaded.

The country all around Fern Falls was beautiful, and a favourite walk was down to the Falls themselves, which were a series of small cascades tumbling down a rocky ravine.

Philip turned their steps this way, and they sauntered along the winding footpath that followed down the side of the falls.

"It is lovely here," said Patty, as she sat down on a rock for a short rest. "But I wouldn't want to live in the country all the year around, would you, Philip?"

"Not if you didn't like it, dear. Suppose we have two homes, one in the city and one in the country?"

"Homes for lunatics, do you mean?" and Patty favoured the young man with a wide-eyed gaze of inquiry.

"You know very well what I mean," and Philip returned her gaze with one of calm regard. "You know why I brought you out here this afternoon, and you know exactly what I'm going to say to you. Don't you?"

"Not EXACTLY," and Patty drew a roguish frown; "they all word it differently, you know."

"It is a matter of utter indifference to me how the others word it," and Philip leaned up comfortably against a rock as he looked at Patty. "The only thing that engrosses my mind, is whether I myself can word it persuasively enough to make you say yes. Do you think I can?"

"You never can tell till you try," said Patty, in a flippant tone.

"Then I'll try. But, Patty, dearest, you know it all; you know how I love you, you know how long I have loved you. Aren't you ever going to give me the least little encouragement?"

"How can I, Phil, when I don't feel encouraging a bit?"

"But you will, dear, won't you? You remember last winter when we went on that sleighride after the butter and eggs? Why, Patty, you ALMOST said yes, then."

"Why, Philip Van Reypen! I didn't do anything of the sort! I had no idea of saying yes, then, - I haven't now, - and I'm not sure that I ever shall have!"

"I'll wait, Patty," and Van Reypen spoke cheerfully. "I'll wait, Little Girl, because I think a love like mine is bound to win at last. And I know you're too young yet to make up your mind. But, Patty, there isn't anybody else, is there?"

"Anybody else what?"

"Anybody else who likes you as much as I do. Is there?"

"Now, Phil, how could I tell that? When people say they love you heaps and heaps, you never know quite how much to believe, or quite how much is just the influence of the moonlight."

"Well, there's no moonlight here now. So when I tell you how much I love you, it's all true. You believe that, don't you, Little Girl?"

"Yes, I believe it. But, Philip, I wish you wouldn't talk about it to-day. I'm tired of -"

"Of having men tell you how much they love you? Poor little Patty! I'm afraid you'll have to put up with that all your life."

"Oh, horrible!" and Patty made a wry face. "I suppose some girls like it, but I don't."

"I'll tell you a way to avoid it, Patty. Be engaged to me, now, - even if you won't marry me right away, and then, you see, other men can't propose to you."

"Do you mean be engaged to you, Phil, without intending EVER to marry you!"

"Well, don't consider the second question at present. Just be engaged to me, and then we'll see about it."

"No, I don't think that would be fair. You make it seem as if being engaged to a man doesn't mean anything."

"Patty! dearest! DON'T talk like that! It would mean all the world to me. And I'm sure I could make you love me enough to want to marry me, after awhile. If you knew how much I loved you, I'm sure you'd agree that you couldn't resist that love for long."

Van Reypen looked very handsome and very earnest as he gazed into Patty's eyes. And Patty looked very sweet and dear as she gazed back at him with a troubled expression on her lovely face.

Then with a sudden, impulsive gesture she put out both her hands and Philip took them in his own.

"Don't make me decide now, Phil," she said, and she looked at him with a pathetic smile. "I don't know what

I want. I know I DON'T want to marry you, - or anybody else, - for a long time. And I don't think I want to be engaged to anybody just yet, either."

"Of course you don't, you dear little girl," and Van Reypen's tone was hearty and genuinely helpful. "You've only just begun to have your little fling, and enjoy yourself in your own sweet, butterfly way. And I'm not going to tease you or cause you one moment's worry. But, oh, Patty, darling, if ever you have a moment when you want to think about these things, think about me, won't you, dear? And remember that my whole heart is yours and my whole life is devoted to you. You don't understand now, what the whole love of a man means, but some day you will, and then, if your heart can turn to me, let it do so, won't you, - little sweetheart?"

Patty was thrilled, not only by Philip's words, but by the deep and sincere love shining in his eyes, and which she could not mistake.

"You are very dear to me, Philip," she said, with absolute sincerity; "and I do want you to know how much I appreciate what you have said, - and how grateful I am -"

"Hush, Patty," and Philip smiled gently at her; "I don't want that. I don't want your appreciation nor your gratitude for what I feel for you. When you are ready to give me your love, in return for the love I offer you, I want it more than I can tell you. But until then, I want your friendship, the same good comradeship we have always had, but not any gratitude, or foolishness of that sort. Do you understand?"

"I do understand, Phil, and I think you're splendid! I want to keep on being your friend, - but I don't want you to think -"

"No, dear; I promise not to think that you are giving me undue encouragement, - for that is what you're trying to say. And you mustn't let my hopes or desires trouble you. Always treat me just exactly as you feel toward me, with gay comradeship, with true friendliness, or whatever is in your heart. But always remember that I am still loving you and waiting and hoping."

Philip gave Patty one long look deep into her eyes, and then, with an entire change of manner, he said lightly, "Now, my lady fair, if you are rested, suppose we walk back to the house?"

"I am rested," and Patty jumped up, "so you won't have to do what I feared, - take me home in a wheelbarrow."

Van Reypen looked at her quizzically.

"Do you remember," he said, "the classic poem from which that quotation is taken?"

"It's from Mother Goose, isn't it?"

"Yes; but if you recollect, it was a bachelor gentleman who went to London. And when he returned he brought a WIFE home in a wheelbarrow. I'm not having quite THAT experience."

"No," said Patty, demurely, "but you haven't any wheelbarrow."

CHAPTER XIX

IN THE RUNABOUT

When they reached the house, Patty went straight up to Mr. Kenerley, and said in a low tone, "Jim, I want to ask a favour of you."

"Anything at all, Patty Pink; anything, to the half of my kingdom!"

"Well, I want the little car, the runabout; and I want to go off for a little while, all by myself."

"Patty! You amaze me! Does this mean a clandestine meeting with a rustic swain? Oh, my child, I thought you were well brought up!"

"Don't tease me, Jim," and Patty looked really serious. "If you must know, though, it's because I want to get away from the rustic swains. I want a little time to myself. And if I stay here, the boys are all around; and if I go to my room, the girls won't give me any peace, and, oh, Jim, DO help me out!"

"Why, of course, you Blessed Infant. Trust all to your Uncle Jim! Come along with me."

The two started down the walk toward the garage, and

Adele called out, "Where are you going?"

"Going to elope," Kenerley returned gaily over his shoulder, and they went on.

He took out the little car, which Patty could easily run herself, and putting her in, he jumped in beside her.

"I'll go with you, past the porch," he said, "and see you outside the gate."

So they dashed by the group on the veranda, not heeding their chaff and once outside the grounds, Jim said, "Are you sure you want to go alone, Patty?"

"Yes, please, Jim. I want to think a little."

"Oh, you GIRL! you needn't tell ME! some chap's been making love to you!"

"Nonsense!" but Patty's blush belied her words.

"I hope it IS nonsense, Patty, dear. You're too young to have a serious affair yet awhile. Take an old friend's advice and say no this time."

"Of course I shall. Don't worry about me, Jim."

"No, indeed. You've good common sense in that curly golden pate of yours. I'll get out here, and you go along, Patty, and have a nice little maiden meditation all to yourself, and come back fancy free, but don't stay out too late."

Kenerley got out of the car and went back to the house, and Patty drove on alone.

It was just what she wanted, an opportunity to think over what Philip had said. And she was fond of motoring alone, and an experienced driver. She went slowly at first, enjoying the beautiful country with its serene air of Sunday afternoon calm.

The trend of her thoughts was not a question of whether or not she should accept Van Reypen; but more a dreamy recollection and living over the scene at the Falls.

She pictured in her mind how really noble and handsome he looked, and she almost wondered at herself why she had only a friendly feeling toward him.

"But I like him better than Kenneth," she assured herself; "that is, I like him MORE than I do Kenneth. Ken is an old dear, but he IS slow; and Philip has all the nice ways and mannerisms that I do like in a man. He's always equal to any occasion, without any effort. He's just born so. He's an aristocrat like his aunt, but he hasn't a bit of her, - well, - it is really a kind of snobbishness. She's intolerant of people not in her own set. But Phil is kind and courteous to everybody. And he has a sense of humour. I suppose that's what's the matter with Ken. The poor boy hasn't a spark of fun in him except what I've banged into his blessed old head. There's Kit Cameron now, he has too much fun in him. He'd make anybody's life a practical joke. I don't believe he half meant what he said to me in the swing last night. I think he would have said the same to any girl, sitting there in the moonlight. Well, I do seem to be growing up. I wish I had Nan here. She's so nice to talk things over with. Not that I want to talk anything over. I believe it isn't considered correct to tell about the proposals you have, but I guess a mother wouldn't count, - even if she is a stepmother. And Nan is such a duck of a stepmother! I'll certainly tell her about these proposals I've had. I don't believe I'll ever have any more. But all the same, I'm not going to get engaged yet! I'd rather be an old maid than to take the first man who asks me. But there's one thing certain, I do like Philip the best of the bunch!"

Patty went on along the highway, stopping now and then to gather a particularly beautiful branch of wild rose, or a few spring beauties.

She had on a simple little frock of pink linen, with a sailor collar of fine white embroidery, and a big black velvet bow at her throat. She wore no hat but her golden hair was partly confined by a band of black velvet. She had a light dust coat of pongee silk, though Jim had told her there was a warmer coat in the car if she should want it.

When Kenerley returned to the group on the veranda a wild shout greeted him, inquiring where Patty was.

"I told you she was going to elope," returned Jim; "I was merely helping her along. I left her just outside the gate on her way to meet her rustic swain."

"Nonsense, Jim," said his wife, "where did she go? Over to the Crosbys'?"

"She didn't say anything to me about the Crosbys. In fact, Adele, she didn't tell me where she was going, and I wasn't so inquisitive as to ask her. I let my guests do as they like and go where they choose. Patty asked me for the runabout and I gave it to her. If she had wanted the touring car she could have had it, - or the limousine, - or the wheelbarrow."

A smile passed over Van Reypen's face at the chance reference to the last-named vehicle, and his intuitions told him that Patty had gone for a solitary drive to get away from other people for a little while.

"Oh, LOOK who's here!" cried Daisy, suddenly, as a motor car came whizzing up the steps and out jumped Bill Farnsworth.

"I just stopped for a minute," he said to Adele, "to see how you all are after your party."

"All quite well," said Adele, "but sorry you couldn't stay here with us instead of going on."

"Sorry, too," said Farnsworth. "Where's Miss Fairfield?" and he looked about inquiringly.

"Gone for a drive," replied Adele, and Farnsworth made no further reference to Patty. But his call was short and soon he was again starting his car.

"Which way did Miss Fairfield go?" he murmured in a low voice to Kenerley, as his car moved off.

"East," said Jim, with a teasing smile at Farnsworth, and then Bill was gone.

He swung out on to the broad highway and turned east. There were no bypaths near and he had an intention of following and overtaking Patty. He wanted to see her, and with Bill Farnsworth to want to do anything was to do it.

Now it chanced that Patty had had a detention. Though an expert driver, and a fairly good mechanician for her own car, she was not entirely familiar with the car she was driving, and when it stopped stock-still at the side of the road, she found herself unable to discover the exact difficulty.

She was not overanxious, for it was a frequented road and she felt sure some car would come along, in whose driver she might feel sufficient confidence to ask help. But it so chanced that she sat for some time before any car came. The sun was warm and she threw off her coat, really enjoying basking in the sunshine while she waited.

And it was this sudden apparition of a golden head shining in the sunlight that gave Farnsworth a shock of surprise as he came up behind Patty's car.

"By Jove!" he exclaimed, "there she is! In trouble, too. Jolly well I came along, bless her heart! But it's funny if she can't manage the car. I believe she's sitting there purposely."

For a few moments Bill sat looking at the yellow head and smiling gently at it. Then he had an inspiration to drive right past her and see if she would speak to him. She had been far from cordial the day before and Farnsworth was uncertain whether she wanted to see him or not.

So, driving slowly, he passed by Patty in her motionless car.

Patty jumped at the sound of some one coming, and intending to ask help , held out her hand and said,

"Please - " before she realised who it was.

Farnsworth turned his head, stopped his car, whipped off his cap and jumped out, saying, as he walked toward Patty's car, "An accident, ma'am? Can I help you?"

A spirit of perversity rose in Patty's heart. Without knowing why, she desired to inflict a hurt on the man who was smiling at her.

"I beg your pardon," she said, coldly, "I thought you were a stranger."

"I'll be a stranger, if you like," and Farnsworth bowed profoundly.

"Very well, I wish you would. Pray proceed with your journey," and Patty bowed, and turned her head toward the opposite landscape.

"But you would ask a stranger to help you," said Farnsworth, feeling a strong desire to shake the exasperating little pink figure.

"Not every stranger," said Patty. "I am waiting to select the one I want."

"Oh, DO select me! I'm an awfully nice stranger, and incidentally, I could fix that car of yours in a jiffy."

"Did Adele order you to fix this car?" and Patty's blue eyes gave Bill a look of withering scorn.

"No, she did not."

"Then I can't think of allowing you to do it. I don't want you to do ANYTHING for me except at Adele's orders!"

"You little goose! I've a notion to kidnap you, wild roses and all, and take you off in my car."

"Did Adele order you to do THAT?"

"Patty, stop this nonsense! Of course I know what you mean, that I asked you to dance in Adele's name, instead of in my own."

"Yes; I admit I prefer to be asked to dance, personally, and not vi-vike -"

"Vicariously is the word you are floundering over," said Farnsworth with utmost gravity; "well, now, I'll fix your car vicariously, or personally, or any old way you like, - if you'll just behave yourself and smile upon me."

"I don't want my car fixed."

"You prefer to stay here?"

"I do."

"Alone?"

"Alone." Patty tried very hard to look like a stone image but only succeeded in looking like a very pretty pink-cheeked girl.

However, at her last word, and when Patty was just about to break into a dimpled smile, Farnsworth achieved a most dignified and conventional bow, replaced his cap, and without another glance at Patty, deliberately got into his car and drove away. He passed Patty, continuing east, and in a few moments was lost to sight, as he flew down the road at a swift pace.

"Well!" remarked Miss Patricia Fairfield, aloud. "Well! Hooray for you, Little Billee! I didn't know you had it in you to act like that! But" - and her face clouded a little - "I suppose your head is so full of Kitty Morton that you don't care what becomes of Patty Fairfield! H'm."

Patty sat still for some time, thinking over this new episode. She had been rude to Farnsworth, and she had done it purposely. But she was accustomed to having young men laugh at her pertness and chuckle over her sauciness.

One or two cars passed her, but as she scrutinised the drivers, they did not seem to be just the type of whom she cared to ask help; but presently a small car came toward her, driven by a frank-looking, pleasant-faced young man.

"Hello," he called out with the camaraderie of the road; "had a breakdown? Want some help?"

"Yes, sir," and Patty spoke in a timid, subdued voice.

"Then I'm your man," he said, as he jumped out and came over to her car. "My name's Peyton," he went on, "Bob Peyton, and very much at your service. What's the matter?"

" I don't know , sir , " and Patty surrendered to a

mischievous impulse; "I'm Mrs. Hemingway's maid; Mrs. Hemingway, sir, she can run the car, but I can't."

"Where is Mrs. Hemingway?"

"When the car broke down, sir, she said she would go for help. I think she went to that house over there."

"H'm! And so you're her maid. Personal maid, do you mean?"

"Not exactly, sir. I'm her new waitress, she was just taking me home, sir."

Patty didn't know why she was talking this rubbish, but it popped into her head, and the young man's eyes were so twinkly and gay, she felt like playing a joke on him. She thought he would fix her car, and then she would thank him and ride away, without having given her real name.

"Ah, my good girl," Mr. Peyton said, "and so you are a waitress. What is your name?"

"Suzette, sir. I'm French."

"Yes, I can see that by looking at you! Well, Suzerte, are you an experienced waitress?"

"Oh, yes, sir. I've worked in the best families and in, - and in hotels and - and -"

"And on oceans liners, I presume! Well, Suzette, here's a proposition. My sister wants a waitress, awfully. Hers has just left. If you will go along with me to my sister's house , she will pay you twice what your previous mistress did."

Patty appeared to consider the question.

"Who is your sister, sir?"

"Mrs. Brewster; she lives in that next place, where you see the red brick chimneys."

Now Patty knew all about the Brewsters, although she had never met them. They were great friends of the Kenerleys, and indeed the whole house party was invited to dine at the Brewsters' the next night. Adele, too, had spoken about Bob Brewster's brother, and Patty realised they were friends and neighbours.

In her present mood, Patty was simply aching for an escapade. And she thought it would be a pretty good practical joke if she should go to Mrs. Brewster's and pretend to be a waitress. She would telephone Adele what she was up to, and they would send another car for her that evening. Perhaps if she had thought another moment she wouldn't have done it, but on the impulse she said. "I'd love to get double wages, sir, and I will go to your sister's, but what about Mrs. Hemingway's car?"

"I will take you over to my sister's first, - it's only a short jump, and then I'll come back and see about this car."

So Patty got out of her own car and into Bob Peyton's, and in a moment they were spinning along toward the red chimneys.

The young man said not a word on the way, and Patty's

spirits fell as she began to think she had undertaken a foolish prank, with no fun in it. But she realised that in her role of waitress she could not expect the young man of the house to talk to her, so she sat demurely silent, trying to look as much like a waitress as possible, and succeeding not at all.

On reaching the house, which proved to be a large and elaborate affair, Mr. Peyton drove around to a side door. He ushered Patty into a small waiting-room, and went in search of his sister. Patty heard much gay laughter from the drawing-rooms, and suddenly felt that her joke was not as funny as she had expected. But she determined to carry it a little further and see what might happen.

A charming young woman soon came to her, and said with a pleasant smile, "Is this Suzette?"

"Yes, madame," and Patty's manner was quite all that was to be desired in a waitress.

"I am Mrs. Brewster. My brother has told me the circumstances of his finding you. I am not sure that I'm doing right in taking you away from your present employer, but I'm going to be selfish enough to ask you to help me out for a short time, anyway. I have guests for dinner, and my waitress has gone. My guests are really important people and I was at my wits' end how to manage, until you appeared. If you will only stay and wait on my table at dinner, I will let you do as you choose afterwards, - return to Mrs. Hemingway or remain with me."

The plan seemed to promise some fun to Patty. She would privately telephone Adele, who would tell Jim.

It was to be a joke on the rest of them, especially Kit who had said Patty could never fool him. And ever since the Belle Harcourt joke, which had not fooled Kit after all, she wanted to try again. She would make Adele pretend she thought Patty was lost, and both Kit and Philip would be greatly alarmed.

"I will stay for dinner, madame," she said, at last, "and afterward we can decide. You may not like my work."

"I'm sure I shall; you seem capable, and my brother tells me you are experienced. I fear though, your gown is a little, - a little -"

"I understand, madame. You see, this is my Sunday afternoon frock. If I stay with you, I will send for my black ones. Perhaps, if I took off the lace collar now."

"Yes, and the black bow. It is those things that make your garb inappropriate. I will, of course, provide you with an apron and cap. Will you come with me now to the dining-room, and I will show you about your duties."

Mrs. Brewster gave Patty full directions about the serving of the dinner and then provided her with a cap and apron. The trifle of muslin and lace, when perched on Patty's gold curls, was really most becoming; and though she removed her collar and bow, the frilled bretelles of the dainty apron were quite as effective, and Patty looked like the kind of waitress that is seen in amateur plays.

"If not asking too much, madame," she said, "may I telephone to a friend?"

"Is it necessary?" and Mrs. Brewster looked a little surprised.

"It would be polite, I think, madame," returned Patty, with eyes cast down, "as it is to some people with whom I expected to take supper. They will wait for me, I fear?"

"Ah, yes, Suzette, you are right. You may telephone, but I will tell you frankly, I do not like to have my servants make a practice of telephoning to their friends."

"No, madame," and Patty's tone was most humble.

To her great delight the telephone was in a small booth by itself, and Patty soon made Adele acquainted with the whole story.

Adele was not altogether pleased with the prank, but as she couldn't help herself, she accepted the situation with a good grace, and promised to send for Patty later in the evening.

CHAPTER XX

THE RIDE HOME

Patty stood in the butler's pantry when the guests entered the dining-room for dinner.

She was determined to do her part perfectly, for she knew quite well how everything should be done, and she entered into the spirit of it as if it were a play.

There were eight at the table, and as Patty tripped in to serve the soup she caught the approving glance of Mr. Bob Peyton. She quickly dropped her eyes and proceeded with her duties quietly and correctly. But as she set down the third soup plate, she chanced to look across the table, and met the calm, straightforward gaze of Bill Farnsworth!

She didn't drop the soup-plate or make any awkward movement. Patty was not that sort. She looked down quickly, though it was with difficulty that she prevented the corners of her mouth from breaking into a smile. Immediately she suspected the whole truth. Farnsworth was a guest at this house, - of course he had sent Bob Peyton to her rescue! Or, hadn't he? Could it have been possible that Mr. Peyton found her unexpectedly? She didn't think so. She believed that Little Billee had sent Peyton to her aid, because she had refused his assistance. Of course, Bill had not foreseen the waitress joke, and doubtless he was as much surprised to see her now as she was to see him. Unless Mr. Peyton had told all the guests that he had found a waitress along the road in a stalled motor-car!

Well, at any rate, Patty determined to go on with the farce to the best of her ability. If Farnsworth thought he could rattle her, he was very much mistaken. But she would not look at him again. If he should smile at her, she knew she should smile, for she was on the verge of laughing anyway. So the dinner proceeded. Patty did her part beautifully, serving everything just exactly right and doing everything just as it should be done. And not once during the long dinner, did she catch the eye of either Farnsworth or Mr. Peyton. Once or twice she looked at Mrs. Brewster with a note of inquiry in her eyes, and that lady gave an almost imperceptible nod of approval, so that Patty knew everything was going all right.

At last it was time for Patty to bring in the finger bowls. They stood neatly ranged in readiness for her, and in each one was a pansy blossom.

On the table near the doorway through which Patty went in and out of the dining-room, chanced to be a big bowl of apple blossoms, and Patty appropriated one of these and substituted it for the pansy in the finger bowl which she subsequently placed before Farnsworth.

She did not glance at him, but she had the satisfaction of seeing him start with surprise, and then let his glance travel around the table as if assuring himself that he was the only one thus honoured.

He tried to catch Patty's eye, but she resolutely refrained from looking at him.

After dinner was over, and the guests returned to the drawing-room, Patty remained in the dining-room, wondering what would happen next.

In a few moments Mrs. Brewster came running out to her.

"You little brick!" she cried; "but, my DEAR child, what MADE you do it?"

"What do you mean, madame?" asked Patty, in her most waitress-like voice.

"What do I mean? You rogue! You scamp! Mr. Farnsworth has told us all about it! I don't know what you mean by this masquerade. But it's over now, and you must come into the drawing-room at once! Take off that apron and cap, and put on your collar and bow again."

"Oh, Mrs. Brewster, I can't go into the drawing-room. All your guests have on their evening things, and this is a morning frock!"

"Nonsense, child, come right along in. You look as sweet as a peach."

"But I say, Ethel," and Bob Peyton bounced out into the dining-room, "Miss Fairfield hasn't had any dinner, herself," and he smiled at Patty. "You see I know all about you. Farnsworth told the whole story. You are miffed with him, I believe, and wouldn't let him help you. So he came right over here and sent me back to help a fair lady in distress. Why you got up that waitress jargon *I* don't know."

"I don't either," and Patty dimpled roguishly at him. "I have an awful way of cutting up any jinks that happen to pop into my head! You'll forgive me, won't you?"

"I never should have forgiven you if you HADN'T!" and Peyton smiled admiringly into the big blue eyes that implored his forgiveness so sweetly.

"You DEAR child," Mrs. Brewster rattled on, "to think you haven't had a mite of dinner! Now I will get you something."

"No, no, thank you," laughed Patty, "I will confess that I ate all I wanted here in the pantry while the dinner was going on. Cook sent up special portions for me, and I had plenty of time to do justice to them."

"I'm glad of that," said Mrs. Brewster, cordially, "and now, Miss Fairfield, come into the drawing-room. I want my guests to know what a little heroine it is who waited on us at dinner. What a girl you are! I've often heard Adele Kenerley speak of you, and I'm so glad to know you. You must come and make me a visit, won't you, to prove that you forgive me for letting you wait on my table?"

"The pleasure was mine," returned Patty, dropping a pretty curtsy. Then they all went to the drawing-room, where Patty was praised and applauded till she blushed with confusion.

Farnsworth stood leaning against the mantel as she entered the room. He waited till the introductions were over and until the hubbub roused by Patty's story had subsided. Then, as she stood beside her hostess, he went over to her, and said, "What is your greeting for me, Miss Fairfield?"

"I gave you my greeting at the table," said Patty, and she flashed a glance at him from beneath her long lashes.

"WAS it a greeting?"

But before Patty could answer, Mrs. Brewster came to her and said in her enthusiastic way, "Oh, Miss Fairfield, I've been telephoning Mrs. Kenerley and telling her all about it! And what DO you think? She says that she and Jim are the only ones over there who know where you are, and they're pretending they don't know, and all the young people are crazy with anxiety!"

"I suppose I ought to go right home," said Patty, "and relieve their anxiety. But I'd like to stay a little while longer. And, yet, I don't want them to know where I've been, until I get there, and tell them myself."

"Let them wait," said Bob Peyton. "It won't hurt them to worry a little. Now, Miss Fairfield, we're going to have some music, and perhaps, - as you're such an angel of goodness to us anyway, - perhaps you'll sing for us."

They all sang in chorus, and some sang solos, and after awhile it was Patty's turn.

She had none of her elaborate music with her, so she told Mrs. Brewster she would sing any songs or ballads that she might happen to have.

They found a book of old songs, which Mr. Brewster declared were his favourites, and Patty sang two or three of those.

Among them was the old Scotch song of "Loch Lomond." Patty had never seen this, but as Mr. Brewster was fond of it he urged her to try it. The song was not difficult and Patty read easily, so she made a success of it. As she came to the lines, "I'll take the high road and you take the low road," she glanced at Farnsworth, with a half-smile.

He did not return the smile, but looked at her steadily and with a slightly puzzled expression.

When the song was over, Farnsworth crossed the room and stood by Patty's side.

"Why do you want to take the high road, if I take the low road?" he asked her, abruptly. He took no pains to lower his tones, and Bob Peyton who stood near heard what he said.

"Because I'm taking the low road, and Miss Fairfield will ride with me, though she won't with you."

Peyton's manner was so light and his smile so gay, that Patty answered in the same key, ignoring Farnsworth's serious face.

"I like to take the road with Mr. Peyton," she answered gaily, "because it leads to such pleasant places," and she smiled at Mrs. Brewster.

"You dear child! You are perfectly fascinating," Mrs. Brewster declared.

"There, there, Ethel, you mustn't tell Miss Fairfield what we all think about her," Peyton interrupted.

And then Patty was called to the telephone.

"You must come home, Patty," Adele's voice said.

"All right, I will, Adele," Patty replied; "but tell me this, does Kit think I'm lost, or anything?"

"No, Patty, he doesn't; but all the rest do. Kit pretends he thinks something has happened to you, but he told me privately that he knew perfectly well that you were all right, and that Jim and I know where you are! Oh, you can't fool HIM. But Mr. Van Reypen is nearly crazy. He says he doesn't think anything dreadful has happened to you, but he thinks you've had a breakdown and can't get home, and he insists on starting out to look for you. If you don't come right away, Patty dear, I can't keep him here much longer!"

"All right, Adele, I'll start at once; truly, I will! Don't send for me. Somebody here will take me over. You know your little runabout is here. I'll come home in that."

"Don't drive it yourself."

"Of course not. Somebody will drive me. I'll be over in fifteen minutes. Good-bye."

Patty hung up the receiver and returned to the drawing-room.

"I must go right straight away," she said, smiling at her hostess. "My joke worked a little too well, and unless I appear they're going to send out a search party after me! I told Adele her little car was here. How did it get here, Mr. Peyton?"

"I went after it and brought it here; instead of taking it to Mrs. Hammersmith's or whatever her name was!"

"You mean Mrs. Hemingway," said Patty, laughing, "my former mistress, who left me in her car to go in search of help."

"Yes," said Peyton. "Wasn't it lucky I came along? You little thought Farnsworth sent me, did you?"

"Indeed I didn't!" and Patty smiled at him, "and will you take me home in that little car? for I promised Adele I'd go at once."

"Of course I will," said Bob Peyton, "if you must go."

So Patty was made ready for her drive and Mrs. Brewster insisted she should wear the warm coat as the evening had grown chilly.

The whole crowd went out on the steps to see Patty off, and Mr. Brewster tucked her in, while Bob Peyton cranked the car.

"All aboard," said Peyton, straightening himself up, at last; and then, somehow, - and Patty never knew how it happened, - somebody jumped into the seat beside her, somebody grasped the steering-wheel, and the little car flew down the road and out at the gate, and even before Patty looked up to see the face of the man beside her, she KNEW it was not Mr. Peyton!

She looked up, and saw smiling at her the blue eyes of Bill Farnsworth.

Mrs. Brewster had tied a chiffon scarf over Patty's hair, and as Patty looked up in Farnsworth's face, the moonlight illumined her own face until she looked more like a fairy than a human being.

"Apple Blossom!" said Big Bill, under his breath. "I never shall find a more perfect name for you than that! Now, tell me what it's all about. Hurry up, we haven't much time."

"But - but I'm so surprised! Why are YOU here, instead of Mr. Peyton?"

"Because I wanted to ride home with you."

"So did he."

Farnsworth shrugged his broad shoulders, as if to say that what Peyton wanted was a matter of utter indifference to him. "Go on," he said briefly, "tell me what it's all about."

"I don't know what you mean! What's all WHAT about?"

"The way you're treating me. The last time I saw you was last winter; at the Hepworths' wedding, to be exact. We were friends then, - good friends. Then I came up here, - yesterday. I threw your own flowers in at your window, and you came and smiled at me and said you were glad to see me. Didn't you?"

"Yes," said Patty, in a faint little voice.

"Yes, you DID. And then, - then, Apple Blossom, when you came down stairs later, playing May Queen, you scarcely looked at me! You scarcely spoke to me! You wouldn't dance with me!"

"But you only asked me because -"

"Don't tell that story again! Because Adele told me to ask you, is utter rubbish, and you know it! That isn't why you wouldn't dance with me. No-sir-ee! You had some other reason, some foolish crazy reason, in your foolish crazy little noddle! Now out with it! Tell me what it is! Own up, Posy-Face. You heard something or imagined something about me, that doesn't please your ladyship, and I have a right to know what it is. At least, I'm going to know, whether I have a right or not. What is it or who is it that has interfered with our friendship?"

Patty looked up at Bill and read determination in his face. She knew it was no time for chaffing or foolishness. So she only said, as she looked straight at him, - "Miss Morton."

"Miss Morton! for Heaven's sake, what DO you mean?"

"The girl you're engaged to."

"The girl I'm engaged to! Patty, HAVE you taken leave of your senses?"

"Well, anyway, if you're not engaged to her, you're terribly in love with her! Your whole life and love is bound up in her!"

"Patty, I've heard there is a lunatic asylum over near Scottsville, and I'm going to take you right straight over there, unless you stop talking this rubbish! Now, if you're still possessed of the power of rational conversation, tell me who is this Miss Morton!"

"Miss Kate Morton, - the lady you're in love with."

Patty's spirits had begun to rise, and as she said this she looked up at Farnsworth, with demure face, but with a mouth dimpling into laughter.

"Kate Morton! Why, I haven't seen her for ten years!"

"Was it a hopeless affection, then? Are you only true to her memory?"

"Patty, BEHAVE yourself! Who mentioned Kate Morton's name to you?"

"Kitty! You always call her Kitty."

Farnsworth chuckled. "Call her KITTY! why, I'd sooner call the Flatiron Building 'Kitty.' It would be about as appropriate."

"Well, anyway, you told Adele that you loved Kitty with all your heart and soul."

A great light seemed to break upon Farnsworth. He looked at Patty for a moment, with slowly broadening smile, and then he burst into irrepressible laughter.

" Oh , Patty ! " he exclaimed, between his spasms of

mirth; "Kitty! oh, Kitty! Patty!"

Patty sat looking at him in stern silence.

"I should think, Mr. Farnsworth, if any one ought to go to a lunatic asylum it might as well be you! You sit there like an imbecile saying, oh, Patty! oh, Kitty!"

"I don't know which I love most, you or Kitty!" and again Farnsworth went off in a roar of laughter.

"I don't care to be mentioned in connection with Miss Morton," and Patty tried her best to look like a tragedy queen.

"But it ISN'T Miss Morton, it's Kitty CLIVE."

"Adele said she couldn't remember her last name. But it doesn't matter to ME whether it's Miss Morton or Miss Clive."

"Oh, DON'T, Patty! You'll be the death of me! Why, Apple Blossom, Miss Clive, - Kitty Clive, - is - my horse!"

Patty hesitated a moment, and then gave in, and laughed too.

"You must be AWFULLY fond of your horse," she said at last.

"I am; Kitty Clive is a wonder, and last summer we rode thousands of miles over the prairies. There NEVER was such a horse as my Kitty! And I remember I DID rave about her to Adele. But Adele

MUST have known what I was talking about."

"No, she didn't. She thought it was a girl, and she told me not to - not to - " Patty floundered a little, and then concluded her sentence, "not to interfere."

"And, so, Apple Blossom, you were cool to me, - you were cruel to me, - you had no more use for me whatever; because you thought I liked another girl?"

"Well - I didn't want to interfere."

"You BLESSED Posy-Face! do you know what this MEANS to me? It means that you CARE -"

"No, I DON'T, Bill! I don't care if you like all the girls in the world. Only, you mustn't like them better than you do me."

"As if I COULD like anybody better than I do you!"

"And then we're friends again?"

"Friends!"

"Yes, friends. Don't you want to be friends with me, Little Billee?"

"Apple Blossom, I want to be to you anything and everything that you will let me be."

"Then we will be friends. Chums and comrades and good, GOOD friends."

Patty put a little pink hand out from the big coat sleeve and Bill clasped it in his great warm hand.

"Chums, - Apple Blossom, - and comrades, and good, GOOD friends!"

Carolyn Wells

Choose from Thousands of 1stWorldLibrary Classics By

Adolphus WilliamWard
Aesop
Agatha Christie
Alexander Aaronsohn
Alexander Kielland
Alexandre Dumas
Alfred Gatty
Alfred Ollivant
Alice Duer Miller
Alice Turner Curtis
Alice Dunbar
Ambrose Bierce
Amelia E. Barr
Andrew Lang
Andrew McFarland Davis
Anna Sewell
Annie Besant
Annie Hamilton Donnell
Annie Payson Call
Anton Chekhov
Arnold Bennett
Arthur Conan Doyle
Arthur Ransome
Atticus
B. M. Bower
Basil King
Bayard Taylor
Ben Macomber
Booth Tarkington
Bram Stoker
C. Collodi
C. E. Orr
C. M. Ingleby
Carolyn Wells
Catherine Parr Traill
Charles A. Eastman
Charles Dickens
Charles Dudley Warner
Charles Farrar Browne
Charles Ives
Charles Kingsley
Charles Lathrop Pack
Charles Whibley
Charles Willing Beale
Charlotte M. Braeme
Charlotte M.Yonge
Clair W. Hayes
Clarence Day Jr.
Clarence E. Mulford

Clemence Housman
Confucius
Cornelis DeWitt Wilcox
Cyril Burleigh
D. H. Lawrence
Daniel Defoe
David Garnett
Don Carlos Janes
Donald Keyhole
Dorothy Kilner
Dougan Clark
E. Nesbit
E.P.Roe
E. Phillips Oppenheim
Edgar Allan Poe
Edgar Rice Burroughs
Edith Wharton
Edward J. O'Biren
John Cournos
Edwin L. Arnold
Eleanor Atkins
Elizabeth Cleghorn
Gaskell
Elizabeth Von Arnim
Ellem Key
Emily Dickinson
Erasmus W. Jones
Ernie Howard Pie
Ethel Turner
Ethel Watts Mumford
Eugenie Foa
Eugene Wood
Evelyn Everett-Green
Everard Cotes
F. J. Cross
Federick Austin Ogg
Ferdinand Ossendowski
Francis Bacon
Francis Darwin
Frances Hodgson Burnett
Frank Gee Patchin
Frank Harris
Frank Jewett Mather
Frank L. Packard
Frederick Trevor Hill
Frederick Winslow Taylor
Friedrich Kerst
Friedrich Nietzsche
Fyodor Dostoyevsky

Gabrielle E. Jackson
Garrett P. Serviss
Gaston Leroux
George Ade
Geroge Bernard Shaw
George Ebers
George Eliot
George MacDonald
George Orwell
George Tucker
George W. Cable
George Wharton James
Gertrude Atherton
Grace E. King
Grant Allen
Guillermo A. Sherwell
Gulielma Zollinger
Gustav Flaubert
H. A. Cody
H. B. Irving
H. G. Wells
H. H. Munro
H. Irving Hancock
H. Rider Haggard
H. W. C. Davis
Hamilton Wright Mabie
Hans Christian Andersen
Harold Avery
Harold McGrath
Harriet Beecher Stowe
Harry Houidini
Helent Hunt Jackson
Helen Nicolay
Hendy David Thoreau
Henrik Ibsen
Henry Adams
Henry Ford
Henry Frost
Henry James
Henry Jones Ford
Henry Seton Merriman
Henry Wadsworth
Longfellow
Henry W Longfellow
Herbert A. Giles
Herbert N. Casson
Herman Hesse
Homer
Honore De Balzac

Horace Walpole	Laurence Housman	Robert Lansing
Horatio Alger, Jr.	Leo Tolstoy	Robert Michael Ballantyne
Howard Pyle	Leonid Andreyev	Robert W. Chambers
Howard R. Garis	Lewis Carroll	Rosa Nouchette Carey
Hugh Lofting	Lilian Bell	Ross Kay
Hugh Walpole	Lloyd Osbourne	Rudyard Kipling
Humphry Ward	Louis Tracy	Samuel B. Allison
Ian Maclaren	Louisa May Alcott	Samuel Hopkins Adams
Israel Abrahams	Lucy Fitch Perkins	Sarah Bernhardt
J.G.Austin	Lucy Maud Montgomery	Selma Lagerlof
J. Henri Fabre	Lydia Miller Middleton	Sherwood Anderson
J. M. Barrie	Lyndon Orr	Sigmund Freud
J. Macdonald Oxley	M. H. Adams	Standish O'Grady
J. S. Knowles	Margaret E. Sangster	Stanley Weyman
J. Storer Clouston	Margaret Vandercook	Stella Benson
Jack London	Maria Edgeworth	Stephen Crane
Jacob Abbott	Maria Thompson Daviess	Stewart Edward White
James Allen	Mariano Azuela	Stijn Streuvels
James Lane Allen	Marion Polk Angellotti	Swami Abhedananda
James Andrews	Mark Overton	Swami Parmananda
James Baldwin	Mark Twain	T. S. Ackland
James DeMille	Mary Austin	The Princess Der Ling
James Joyce	Mary Cole	Thomas A. Janvier
James Oliver Curwood	Mary Rowlandson	Thomas A Kempis
James Oppenheim	Mary Wollstonecraft	Thomas Anderton
James Otis	Shelley	Thomas Bailey Aldrich
Jane Austen	Max Beerbohm	Thomas Bulfinch
Jens Peter Jacobsen	Myra Kelly	Thomas De Quincey
Jerome K. Jerome	Nathaniel Hawthrone	Thomas H. Huxley
John Burroughs	O. F. Walton	Thomas Hardy
John F. Kennedy	Oscar Wilde	Thomas More
John Gay	Owen Johnson	Thornton W. Burgess
John Glasworthy	P.G.Wodehouse	U. S. Grant
John Habberton	Paul and Mable Thorn	Valentine Williams
John Joy Bell	Paul G. Tomlinson	Victor Appleton
John Milton	Paul Severing	Virginia Woolf
John Philip Sousa	Peter B. Kyne	Walter Scott
Jonathan Swift	Plato	Washington Irving
Joseph Carey	R. Derby Holmes	Wilbur Lawton
Joseph Conrad	R. L. Stevenson	Wilkie Collins
Joseph Jacobs	Rabindranath Tagore	Willa Cather
Julian Hawthrone	Rahul Alvares	Willard F. Baker
Julies Vernes	Ralph Waldo Emmerson	William Makepeace
Justin Huntly McCarthy	Rene Descartes	Thackeray
Kakuzo Okakura	Rex E. Beach	William W. Walter
Kenneth Grahame	Richard Harding Davis	Winston Churchill
Kate Langley Bosher	Richard Jefferies	Yei Theodora Ozaki
L. A. Abbot	Robert Barr	Young E. Allison
L. T. Meade	Robert Frost	Zane Grey
L. Frank Baum	Robert Gordon Anderson	
Laura Lee Hope	Robert L. Drake	